IMBALANCE

The Quinn Larson Quests Book 4

P.A. WILSON

FREE EBOOK

Claim your copy of Spells and Other Charms when you use the QR code to sign up for my newsletter and learn more about Quinn and Cate's past.

"Quinn, we aren't getting anywhere." Dionne's voice pulled my attention away from the sight of Lionel's body lying on the sofa. Having my sight back was a benefit, but there were some things I could live without seeing. Lionel's lifeless body was one of those things. His lanky frame looked skeletal without life giving it purpose. His red hair looked flat rather than the wild mess it normally ended up in.

"If you don't concentrate, we won't get him back." She poked me, and I came close to telling her that the apprentice doesn't hurt the master, but she was right, and I'm not that kind of wizard. Her hair was drawn back into a ponytail, and she seemed to have aged in the last week beyond her seventeen years. Her green eyes blazed out of dark rings of exhaustion.

"Okay, let me cover him, and then I won't be distracted." I broke the circle and placed a blanket over his body, gently as though he was still sleeping rather than empty. I had no idea whether he felt the cold or not, but it made me feel like I was doing something to help. It had been three days and we hadn't been able to find any spells that would bind Lionel's spirit back to his body.

At least he didn't look, or smell, like he was decomposing. "The spell you used on his body is holding well." I tried to touch his cheek, something I failed to resist doing daily. I couldn't make contact with his skin. There was something encasing him, probably the spell that slows time.

"For heaven's sake, Quinn, snap out of it." Dionne pulled the back of my shirt and dragged me back to the circle. "He'll be fine long enough for us to get it solved, but only if you help. I don't know enough magic to do this alone." She twisted her ponytail into a knot behind her neck and rubbed at her eyes. Even at her age, the stress was starting to take a toll.

I had to admit, she was right. This wasn't like it was with Cate. Lionel wasn't dead. "Okay, let's get this done." I wasn't going to let the hopelessness take over. "You know what we need to do? We'll take a break after this."

"We can keep working," she said. "We don't need to stop."

I knew too well the danger of doing magic when you are tired. Dionne was young. She might be able to go longer than me, but she was also inexperienced. "We'll take a break. There's no point burning ourselves out. We have time. Like you said, Lionel will be fine for a while."

"Quinn, I—"

"No. This time I mean it. Finish the preparation. Maybe this will be the time we get what we need." I gave her the look I remembered hating from my training days. The one that promised serious, but unspecified, repercussions for not obeying.

She nodded and closed the circle again. "Yeah, everyone we asked said the only answers would be found in the circle. They just didn't know what we were supposed to do in the circle. Too bad Fionuir couldn't tell us how she found the spells."

I laughed. "I'm not sure anyone would have gotten the answer out of her even if she could help us. Fionuir will do anything she can to punish me for imprisoning her." Well maybe punish was too soft a word.

Dionne sat across from me, and then tossed the candy and precious stones into the center. "Okay, what's next?"

I smoothed the dirt testing for any contamination. I didn't want any mystery voices or killing spells to surprise us. Nothing seemed to be lurking, and the magic was almost fully returned from the bedrock where I'd sent it for the social worker's inspection. That brought a memory from our last meeting with Ms. Metcalfe and her comment about Dionne's age. "Dionne, when is your birthday?"

"Uh, why?" She studied the packed dirt beneath her.

"How do you avoid answering my questions? The oath you took should make you answer."

She shrugged. "I was going to answer. I just wondered why? Maybe the oath is more patient than you are."

The oath wasn't sentient. "I want to know how long we need to worry that Ms. Metcalfe is going to drop by."

"Oh, yeah, it's in two months. I've already told Ms. M that I'll be leaving school when I turn eighteen."

I created a small circle between us, hoping it would contain any danger. "Aren't you close to graduation?"

"Who cares? I'll be able to learn magic full time. Lionel can help make a room for me upstairs, and we can be a real coven, or whatever we're called."

I looked up to see that she was focused on the candy wrappers. "It would be a waste for you to quit school."

She looked up at me. "But I get to move in here, right?"

I dreaded the thought of having two apprentices living with me, especially one who seemed to find loopholes in her oath so easily. "That's the usual arrangement."

Her smile was a contrast to the worry that had tightened her face. "Great. I can probably start moving some of my stuff in over the next couple of months."

I agreed. "But you are not moving in until you are free of the system."

She picked up the candy and tossed it between her hands. "Yeah. Now let's get to it. Who are we going to call?"

I figured Ranseed would be our best bet since he knew who Lionel was and maybe would care about him, at least as much as a spirit can care about anything. "Okay, this inner circle won't let anything out, but you can put things in. Place two of the candies there and call for Ranseed."

Dionne did as I instructed. At least when it came to magic, she was willing to obey. She whispered the spirit's name. "Will he come right away?"

I gestured for her to be silent. We listened for a few minutes and then a faint sound of rustling leaves came to us. "Remember your question. He is likely to try to get something more than the candy, or give you useless answers."

She nodded and called his name again. Suddenly the rustling noise changed to a roar of pain and then silence.

Dionne opened her mouth, but I held up my hand. If Ranseed was angry, we needed to be sure he was in the circle before asking questions. If he wasn't there, our questions would float through the spirit world, and that meant anyone could answer. The way our luck was running lately, it would probably be a killing demon. Or that voice.

"Why have I been summoned?" his voice came just before a little whirl of dust disturbed the earth. Ranseed rarely showed visual evidence of his presence. I'd always known him as a whirl of dust and a variety of noises. He always displayed his mood as sound, and by the choice this time, he was curious.

Dionne sat straighter and looked to me for direction. I nodded.

She leaned toward the center. "We have questions of a magical nature."

The dust changed shape and seemed to point at Dionne. "Who are you?"

"Quinn's apprentice." She kept her voice even and seemed calm. I was proud of her composure.

Rustling filled the circle before Ranseed croaked out, "Not Lionel, but something more than an apprentice."

"Yes, I am not Lionel." She smiled. I saw her take control of the urge to look at Lionel. She was right to do so. Ranseed might not show it, but he could see what was going on around the circle.

"What is your question?"

I tensed. We'd rehearsed how to ask the question, and if Dionne followed the plan, it would be fine. If she did her own thing... well I wasn't sure what would happen.

"We are looking for a spell to bring a body and spirit together." She was sticking with the plan.

After a long pause, Ranseed said, "There is one. What will you pay for it?"

She looked at me, and I motioned for her to continue. "What price do you want?"

He laughed. "These candies and four favors."

Dionne narrowed her eyes. "No, the candies and one favor."

"Three."

Dionne smiled. "Three candies and one favor. Agreed."

"No, that is not what I said."

"You said three. You didn't say what three. Now what is the spell?"

I was impressed. Dionne was almost as good at negotiating as a druid.

"This spell can be found in the library of Alexander at—"

"No, not the location, the spell."

"I cannot tell you the spell. It is too complex."

Dionne glanced at Lionel's body. "Where is this library?"

"Hmm, it is not so much where, as when. It is in Abyssinia. It was destroyed three thousand years ago."

"Then it is of no use to us. The deal is not valid." Her tone gave no room for him to argue.

"Why do you need this spell? Are you dealing in necromancy?" The dust whirled into a tight column.

I watched her body tighten as the words came out. "No. The spirit of a friend has been separated from his body. He is not dead."

Was Dionne worried about giving too much information? Or hiding pain about Lionel?

"You wish a spell to reunite the friend? Who is this friend?"

She looked at me. I shook my head. There was no need to give him any information on the hope he'd be able to help. If he had anything useful, he would have given it for the favor.

"It doesn't matter. Please leave so we can contact someone with more information."

Good move on her part. If Ranseed was holding back, a knock at his pride would loosen his tongue.

"Before I leave, I have a message for Lionel of the one name." Ranseed's voice was like a rattle of bones.

"Lionel is not available." Dionne was good at diverting questions. I started to see how she managed to get what she wanted from everyone.

"Hmm, it is curious that he is indisposed. I would tell him that there is rumor that his time is coming."

"I'll tell him." Dionne looked at me and shrugged. "Goodbye."

We cleared the circle.

"What the hell was that about?"

"Who knows? It's hard to say what Ranseed might know about Lionel's future." I glanced over at Lionel's body. "You did well."

She blushed. "Thanks. So, who should we call next?"

"No one. If Ranseed didn't know, then no one else will, or no one on that plane. Let's eat, we'll think of something else."

Dionne lost the pale, drawn look as she finished the sandwich I'd made her. I felt ready to pour more of my energy into the circle. Maybe an older spirit, one I wouldn't normally summon, would give us answers. "We need to summon some other spirits."

She looked at me. "What do you mean? I thought Ranseed was our only chance." Along with the color returning to her face, there was a glimmer of hope.

"There are others, but I don't go after them often. The price they ask is usually too high to make any deal worthwhile."

"But if it will save Lionel..." she said.

"Yes, then the price will probably be worth it." I started to clear away the remnants of the meal. Dionne rose to help me. I could tell she still had something to say. It was odd that she didn't just blurt it out.

"Quinn," Dionne said with ill-concealed fear. "If we don't find the answer today, I can make arrangements to stay over. I don't have to go home."

"I know you want to help. I would give everything to get

Lionel back, but we can't make the mistake of risking your ability to practice."

She sighed. "Exactly, I should be here more often. I've told my foster parents that I need to study more, that I might have to stay overnight with a friend."

"No. You know we can't risk having Ms. Metcalfe come by. And you know she will. She seems determined to make a success story out of you."

"But—"

"No buts. Don't lie to your foster parents, or your teachers, or Ms. Metcalfe. While you are in foster care, you need to be extra careful."

"Fine, let's get back to it since I only have a few more hours."

I checked the clock. "You have six more hours. Leave the dishes," I said. She was right, even if she'd exaggerated. We didn't have all day. I needed her to help with the magic because it would drain me too fast. The chores could wait until Lionel was back with us.

My phone rang as she picked through the candy bowl for more spirit bait. I looked at the caller ID.

"Speak of the devil and the devil appears. Or in this case, the social worker." I braced myself and accepted the call. "Ms. Metcalfe, I'm surprised to hear from you on a Saturday."

"I wish I didn't have to work on the weekend, Mr. Larson. But some things simply don't fit into the normal work week."

I glanced at Dionne. She looked like she was waiting for the blade to fall on her neck. I would have to get the details from her, if Ms. Metcalfe didn't just tell me. I had to balance my need to keep the social worker away from the house with my need to get her off the phone. "What can I do to help you?"

"I'm sorry to say that Dionne's school work is suffering due to this job. In the short time she's worked for you, she has missed the deadline on three assignments."

I glared at Dionne, but couldn't blame her when I was the one who needed her. "I see." Whatever Ms. Metcalfe wanted, I wasn't going to offer an opinion. I was supposed to be Dionne's employer, and I imagined that the normal employer wouldn't be all that ready to get involved.

"I will need to review her work schedule with you. Are you available on Monday?"

I gritted my teeth and tried to think of an answer that would keep her away from us forever. I didn't think she would believe that Dionne had quit, and it was too easy to check. "My day is full. Can we make it later in the week?"

"It does need to be sooner rather than later. How is Tuesday?" She wasn't going to be deterred. "I'm afraid it is important. Perhaps it will be okay to email me her schedule for the next month before we meet."

I couldn't remember if Dionne was supposed to be here today, and I didn't have a schedule for her. There was only so much I could do to make this fake employment seem real. "I can do that on Monday, if that's acceptable?"

She agreed and gave me her email address. "I will need to meet with you, Mr. Larson. Dionne was on her way to university before she decided to take on this job. I would hate for her to lose that future."

I really wanted to tell her that I wasn't responsible for every problem in Dionne's life. That I had a life to save, and a prophecy to solve, and her need for petty details was getting in the way of far more important things. "I'm sure Dionne will refocus. If this job is really getting in the way of her future, I can always find someone else to do the work." Dionne's face went white at my words. I shook my head and a little color returned.

"Oh, I don't think it will come to that. She enjoys her work." There was a reluctance in Ms. Metcalfe's voice that surprised me. Why did she keep trying to interfere if she thought Dionne should keep the job?

This felt like a good place to end the call, before I got in too deep. "Okay, well, I hope you have some time to relax this weekend. I need to get back to work. No rest for me either." I waited until she hung up before I ended the call.

I turned to Dionne. "We need to get this sorted out."

She shrugged. "I'll put a schedule together that she'll be happy with."

Was I like that as a teenager? She didn't seem to have any grasp of the fact that her behavior had consequences, let alone any fear of consequences. Maybe it was the result of living amongst the humans. "No, we need to find a way to balance your lessons here with your lessons at school. What's going on? Do you need to spend more time on your school work?"

"No." She swallowed. "Okay. I was spending time with my friends. I can't just ignore them. I guess I lost track of the time I spent with them. I'll make up the assignments."

Frustrated, I clenched my fists to avoid escalating this into an argument. "Yes, you will. When we've got Lionel back, you'll spend half your time here on school work and half on magic. We cannot risk discovery."

"What about getting me ready for the prophecy?" I could hear the strain of trying to sound cool in her voice.

There was no way to fix this. No real answer while we were in the middle of getting Lionel back. There were too many things that were absolutely important right now. "It won't be for long. You'll be out of the system soon, and the prophecy can't be that urgent. I think we'd see some signs if it was, and you would have been contacted by the others." I realized that I was trusting that she would tell me if she had been contacted, and then I became uneasy at the thought that she was very good at hiding things from me. "You haven't heard from anyone, have you?"

She shook her head. "I would have told you. I wish I wasn't a foster child. Maybe if I wasn't in the system, it would be easier to do this."

I couldn't be angry at her trying one more tactic to get me on her side. It was true, but if she wasn't in the system, I wouldn't be her teacher. "If your parents had survived, they would have raised you as a witch. You wouldn't be my apprentice."

"Yeah, I guess." She sat up straight and gave me a smile. "No point in wishing for the past to change. Let's get Lionel back, and then we'll have more control of our time."

I could only hope she was right. I couldn't help but feel like we were never going to get back to normal. This state of emergency was lasting so long that I didn't really remember what it was like before. The feeling of impending crisis was becoming my normal mood. "Okay, we'll try some more risky things now. I will do the summonings. You need to be silent, no matter what happens."

"Why can't I help?" Disappointment tinged her words. She'd been expecting to do everything. I guessed I wasn't the only one who needed time to get used to the fact that I could see.

"Would you accept, just because I said you can't?"

She laughed. "Should I? Is that what a good apprentice would do? Is that how you plan to get me ready for the prophecy?"

"Sometimes it would be nice to have a compliant apprentice," I said, glad we were at the teasing point. "I will do the magic, because I'm going to tap into some deep old spirits. They are hard to reach and highly unpredictable. If they know you are there, they will try to influence you to take their side in some games of power you won't understand."

"How do you know I won't understand?" Her annoyance was clear. She thought it was because she was young.

"Because I don't understand them." I went to a cupboard and reached into the far corner, pulling out a black jar sealed with an inch of wax.

"Who are they?" She took the jar from me. "I thought I just managed a spirit. Isn't Ranseed old?" She was curious now. I worried that she would be curious enough that she'd go looking on her own. Most apprentices didn't have the power to get to these beings without a master. I worried that Dionne would have enough power, and that she wouldn't have enough wisdom to stay away.

I didn't want to pique her interest with a ban on trying the magic. For a change, I could be grateful that we had so many deadlines. I kept it to the facts. "Not this old. These spirits, well I call them that, but I'm not really sure what kind of being they are, they are more ancient than the elementals. They play dark games of power that sometimes reach these planes."

My ploy must have worked because her voice was casual as she asked, "How do you know them?"

I needed to end this conversation and get us back to the workshop. I opened my mouth to tell her exactly that, but before I could answer the room became icy cold. A wailing came from an invisible, distant pain. The desolation of the sound raised tears in Dionne's eyes and froze my heart.

"Quinn, I thought I was the most powerful being you knew," The Morrigan's voice scratched across my nerves.

3

I turned, hoping she would still be in her crow form when I looked. I didn't need any of these interruptions. At this rate, Dionne would have to go home before we drew another circle, let alone actually got any information.

My hope wasn't realized. As I completed the turn, the heat of desire seared my skin. She was in her human form, a woman, milky skin, ebony hair cascading to her thighs, large ripe breasts. I started to count to a million to keep my libido in check – it only partially worked. "Morrigan, how can I be of service?" Maybe she wouldn't take offense and just tell me.

"I am happy that you can see me. Did you miss this?" She ran her hand over her hips and leaned toward me, willing, ready, and...

There was something different this time. Yes, I was aroused, and the room seemed ten degrees too warm for comfort, but I could still think, barely. It had been easier when I was blind. It was too bad that I hadn't realized and enjoyed the minimal break from her power. Knowing that she used her aspects to muddy my mind, didn't give me any power to stop the reaction. "You are desirable whether I can see you or not, and you know it."

She chuckled. The sound bubbled through my veins, and I wondered if I'd imagined that her power was weaker. "I miss you, wizard."

I could hear Dionne fidgeting behind me. Determined to get back to the circle, I took the chance that I would survive hurrying The Morrigan. "Dionne and I have business, Morrigan. While I enjoy our encounters, Lionel needs to be made whole."

"Yes. Dionne, she is the center of many storms," The Morrigan said, her voice sliding from pure sex to terror as her body melted into the crow.

Now I only had to deal with blood freezing fear. I heard Dionne suck in a breath, so it seemed she wasn't immune to either aspects of The Morrigan. Something had changed, before her only emotion seemed to be curiosity.

It was dangerous to press The Morrigan, well any elemental really, but I could feel time draining away. "Do you need something, Morrigan?"

She slid into her woman form, this time an older version, still attractive, but not blindingly so. "I need many things, Quinn Larson. Perhaps you will learn of all my needs soon. Or perhaps I will continue to allow you to speak to me in such a disrespectful way."

I put an apologetic look on my face, hoping it was sincere because no matter what I wanted, she was powerful enough to stop me permanently. "Is there anything I can do to be of service to you, Morrigan?"

Her gaze slid over me, but that normal feeling of desire was absent. I felt assessment, and disappointment. "I may have information for you. I have not yet decided what I will ask as payment. You are so far in my debt already that I fear you will have to live forever."

"I hope so," Dionne whispered.

I would have to deal with her comment later. Even if it was

only on graduation as an apprentice, she would need to handle leaving me. Losing her parents probably made it hard for her to think about losing anyone, and having her world completely changed overnight could have made her cling to me and Lionel too much. But that was not the topic for today. "I live to make you happy," I said, then regretted the tone as The Morrigan's eyes narrowed.

"Sarcasm is not as amusing as you think, wizard." She flickered between crow and temptress again. "I have taken souls off the battlefield who were more respectful than you."

"I was being sincere."

She raised an eyebrow, but seemed to be willing to let it go. "All of the six are alive. This is the time for the prophecy to ripen. We will remember this as the time before."

"Before what?" Dionne blurted out.

I stopped myself from reacting. The Morrigan didn't need to know, or perhaps didn't need confirmation of what she suspected, that I was not in control of my apprentices.

The Morrigan flicked her hand at Dionne. "I do not know the details. But there will be change. A prophecy this powerful is never subtle in its blossoming."

It looked like we were in for a long visit. "Can we offer you refreshment?" It would give Dionne something to do, other than interrupt.

The Morrigan's attention returned to me, along with a sinking sensation. Not quite terror, more like the aftermath, when you've given in to the inevitable and are preparing to move to the next plane. "No. Despite the pleasant conversation, I have not come to visit. I have come to tell you of my vision."

When I met The Morrigan, I had thought she was one of the first beings, a goddess. Over the years, I had come to realize she was only one of many elemental forces in the world. She was our aspect of the power of life and death. Each religion, or culture had a version, but none were the original. Kali, Freya, Proserpina, they were all aspects of an older more powerful being. One of the creatures I was going to summon – perhaps summon was not the right word – to our circle when The Morrigan left us. All of these aspects had limitations, despite their pretense of omnipotence. The Morrigan's was that she could feel the future, but not see it.

I motioned for Dionne to sit and joined her on the couch. The Morrigan lounged on a chair across from us.

"It came to me as I wandered a prison in Texas. The death row inmates are grateful for my ministrations, even if they only see me in their dreams." She smiled, making me wish I was one of the men waiting for my death. "I saw only light in my vision, but I felt the truth coming."

"How do you know what the vision is telling you?" Dionne's tone was respectful enough to make The Morrigan pause.

After a moment, she responded. "It must be difficult to have an apprentice around you every day, Quinn. Do the questions ever stop?"

"If they do, it usually means something is about to explode, or collapse. While they are asking, they are not doing." I patted Dionne's shoulder in reassurance. "Would you be kind enough to provide an answer?"

She leaned forward almost purring in pleasure. "I am feeling indulgent today, so yes. I have visions constantly, Dionne. The death of every soul is a vision to me. I see their deaths and the path they must follow afterward. Each is a light that trembles in my mind. In that light, I know the name and fate of the soul."

She waited, watching Dionne, but no further questions came. "I have prophetic visions rarely, but when I do, the light blinds me. Voiceless sounds fill my mind pouring their meaning into me. I am frozen in whatever form I inhabited when the vision came."

"What meanings did you get this time?" Dionne was leaning forward, her focus on The Morrigan, curiosity driving away all the other emotions.

"The meaning was as I said, the truth is coming. I can only say this truth has the feeling of potential for great pain and great joy. I have no other answers for you." She shimmered and settled to the crow form. Along with the bird came cold, and wailing, and a feeling as though I should be in pain, but no pain. The crow raised her wings and I rushed to open the window so she could leave. Although when she came to us the windows were closed.

Then we were alone.

I closed the window and rubbed warmth into my arms. Dionne was already up and heading to the basement door. I saw her wipe her eyes, but knew she wanted that to be private.

Determined this time to start our summoning, I followed. "Okay, before anyone else interrupts us, let's get downstairs."

She turned to say something, but the doorbell chimed before she could get any words out.

I was tempted to pretend we were not home. If we ignored the ringing, the interruption might go away. Dionne looked at me, and I could see the same thought cross her mind as her eyes shifted from the basement door to the front of the house.

As much as I wanted to go to the workroom and draw a circle, I knew that whoever was at our door wasn't going away when the bell rang again and the ring didn't stop. I motioned Dionne to stay where she was and made my way down the hall, rehearsing the words I'd use to send the ringer away.

Opening the door, I looked into the hood of a druid. The only lone druid I knew was Myrddin. I stepped onto the porch and glanced along the street. It was empty.

"I was not seen, Quinn. May I enter?"

He was being extraordinarily polite. Usually, he simply ordered me to do his bidding. As I looked, he smiled. It was almost as unnerving as The Morrigan's smile, and nowhere near as inviting.

"What do you want?"

His smile wavered. "To speak with you about your apprentice, Lionel."

Now I couldn't deny him entrance. What if he had something that would help? "Fine, come into the kitchen. Dionne is here, so be prepared to answer questions without expecting to get anything in return."

I was surprised when he nodded. Druids valued information almost as much as others valued life. I had something to look forward to, an uncomfortable druid.

When we settled in the kitchen, I motioned for Myrddin to start. He looked toward the kettle, but I was in no mood to be a host. The sooner he finished his business, the sooner we would be back with Lionel. This was the last interruption I was going to allow.

Myrddin cleared his throat and settled into a professorial pose. "We are aware of your predicament. We are concerned that Lionel's spirit now resides in the amulet with those brothers we lost so long ago. We fear that his presence is causing disturbance. We—"

Dionne sat bolt upright. "Then help us get him out." There was an edge of power in her voice that gave me pause. When she came fully into her magic, it would be hard for anyone to make her do anything.

Myrddin winced. "Your apprentice lacks the proper attitude."

I bristled at his attempt to correct her. "Dionne's attitude is acceptable in this situation." I would talk to her later about holding her temper. "What did you want to say about Lionel?"

He glanced at the door to my basement. I almost invited him to see Lionel, then realized he was trying to influence me with magic. Now my anger was up. This was a new approach, and it was unacceptable. If he wanted the proper attitude from us, he'd better be prepared to show some respect for me. "Myrddin, you are not going to get access to my workroom." If he had information, it was time to spill it. If not, I was going to ban him from my home and make sure that Dionne had no authority to give him access in the future. "Speak or leave."

He nodded. A shadow of apology crossed his face before he retreated further into the hood of his jacket. "Please excuse my curiosity. I have never seen a body that survives being separated from the spirit. In my experience, the body dies quickly unless a new soul can be found to animate it."

I was not interested in reanimating Lionel. If we couldn't fix him, we would release the spell that held his body in time, and bury him. It would hurt, but it would be the right thing to do. "You came here to say something about Lionel," I prompted.

"Yes. We have searched our library to no avail. I was not surprised that we found nothing. We have searched for a way to release the souls of our brothers in vain. I thought that we could discuss a way to calm the souls regardless of Lionel's fate."

I counted to ten. It barely worked enough to stop me from dragging him out of the house. He'd interrupted us for no reason. It was too soon to be thinking of anything but finding a way to undo what Dionne had done to save Lionel. Despite having to keep my temper to a non-violent level, I was curious. What did the druids think would be a good solution? "When this began, you were convinced that Fionuir's imprisonment was the cause of the unrest. Then the prophecy. What is your new theory?"

"You have every right to be cynical," Myrddin said in a rare show of humility. "People expect the druids to know everything. Because we are the keepers of so much knowledge, they think we are familiar with every line of text and spell diagram. Some of the knowledge we hold is ancient, some unintelligible due to age and wear. Some of it is simply not usable because power has changed in the millennia since magic became more than an oral tradition."

Save me from the long-windedness of scholars. "Do you have any information that will help?"

Dionne spoke while Myrddin considered what to say in answer. "Quinn, I think he is hinting that we should kill Lionel's body."

Myrddin patted the air with his hands. "No, do not say kill.

We think of it as releasing the pain his spirit feels at the constant desire to return to its body, without a tether to find its way back."

I didn't understand what he could mean except that we should kill Lionel. No matter what he called it, that's what it would feel like. "So, this is your latest theory. That Lionel is causing the souls to stir?"

"No, that is not what we would call a theory. We suspect, but without a way to enter the amulet we cannot possibly know the truth. What we do know is that the pain of the souls in the amulet will not be contained by the stone. It will leak into the environment that we inhabit. People will begin to feel the agony and despair."

"How do you know that?" Dionne asked. "You want us to kill Lionel based on information you give us, but you won't tell us anything that feels like proof."

"You do not trust us?" He sounded truly surprised. "Perhaps it is because you were not raised in our world. Druids are holders of knowledge arcane. Real Folk have trusted us without question as far back as any of us can remember."

I let her continue on that vein. Myrddin was right, I might have a biased view. I could feel myself fighting a battle between my distrust of Myrddin and my conditioned respect for the knowledge held by the druids.

Dionne snorted her opinion of his argument. "You are right. I was taught to look for proof rather than just blindly believe what I'm told. So, can you give us some kind of proof? Because I am not going to let Lionel die." Her voice hitched on the last words.

Myrddin withdrew. His body was still present, but there was a blankness of his being. The silence continued long enough for me to feel like reaching over and shaking him. Then he looked up at us. "The council understands your reluctance to allow Lionel to pass from this world. We will turn our efforts to finding this proof. We must all hope that it does not come too late."

My impatience took over. I stood. "We need a bit of luck.

Perhaps we will have retrieved Lionel's spirit before you run out of time." I escorted him to the door. As I shut it behind him, I tried to make that wish for luck stronger than just a wish. I couldn't affect the balance of the universe, but surely it was time for things to go right for us. Since Cate's death all of my luck had been bad.

4

I hustled Dionne downstairs before someone else could get between us and our next spell. If we didn't keep trying, we would never get the answer. Or rather, we wouldn't get the answer before the druids found a way to get their solution in place. I wasn't sure I could find the strength to deny the entire grove of druids anything.

Dionne was shaking. She looked to me and I saw tears forming. "Quinn, please tell me you won't let them kill Lionel." I'd never heard her sound so helpless. She was usually so confident that I had to restrain her from doing something foolish.

"Of course we won't. Start drawing the circle." I pointed to the jar of salt. I was on the verge of joining her in her tears. I don't know if it was The Morrigan's visit, or Myrddin's, or both, but I couldn't get rid of the feeling that we were doomed.

Dionne took a handful of salt and started walking around the perimeter of the floor. "What if Myrddin is right? What if people start going crazy?"

I dug out two cinnamon sticks and a mandrake root, powerful aids for the magic we were about to perform. "We'll deal with it if we must. We don't need to anticipate problems. We need to focus on what we're doing."

"Shouldn't we be prepared for it to happen?" She looked away from the salt and it caused a kink in the line.

Fear chilled me. If there was any weakness in the confining circle, the beings summoned could escape to the world. That had been how the demon she'd accidentally called had found Cate. I looked at her and kept my voice calm as I said, "Dionne, clean that up and start again. You need to focus, or we won't be able to contain whatever responds."

She paled even more as I said the words, making me regret the choice. "Sorry. I would hate to make that mistake again."

I didn't say anything. She knew that it wasn't her fault, and hearing it from me again wouldn't make her any less likely to doubt herself.

She put the salt still in her hand back into the container and muttered the words to retrieve the rest from the soil. When the spell had cleared the salt, she returned to the starting place. It would be good if we could do that with salt that had contained a circle. Anything used to confine a spell was changed in some way. The salt was still useful for seasoning, but it wouldn't protect a circle more than once.

I kept my comments to myself as she walked the perimeter of the dirt muttering the spell and letting salt run from her fingers. She had a knack for knowing just how much to take from the jar. She never seemed to run out before the spell was placed. As she started the last part of the incantation, I returned to my task.

She knew to leave a gate that we'd close when we had everything we needed.

I was grateful to have a moment or two when I didn't have to worry about her. I needed to clear this melancholy that seemed determined to take hold. Intellectually, I knew that the emotions we took into the circle could have an effect on the summoning.

Emotionally, I struggled to find a less dark side to the events, let alone a bright side. I owed it to Dionne to get this right. As I picked through the ingredients, I did the same through my memories, finding bright images of joy, and warm images of love. By the time she was done, I felt, at least, calm. Hopeful was still out of reach.

"Okay," she said. Her voice was dull, making me look up from my search for petrified wood. Her skin lacked the usual glow, making her look as though she hadn't slept in far too long. Was she feeling the effects of the amulet? Was I going to get paranoid at every mood swing of a teenage girl?

Still fighting to hold onto the calm, I tried to cheer her up. "Dionne, it will be okay. I just have a feeling we'll get this right."

She glanced away from the salt and grinned. "As long as you have a feeling." Her laugh heartened me and did more to break the despondency than any memory.

The flicker of hope brightened as I pushed the unneeded items to the side. "We'll get this right, and then we'll start on the prophecy."

She placed the jar of salt on the bench beside the pile of dried parsley. "Yeah, I guess it's one of those darkest before the dawn moments, right?"

I wanted to say yes, but I knew that you couldn't know when something was the darkest until it was all done. I felt my grip on calm slipping. Before we were soaked in misery again, I said, "Are you ready?"

She nodded and motioned for me to enter the circle before taking a small handful of salt to close it.

TWO HOURS LATER, WE SAT FACING EACH OTHER, HANDS touching, eyes closed, still trying to get someone or something to answer our call. I opened my eyes as the energy I'd sent into the circle bounced back without response. The light outside was fading, and I needed to finish this last attempt so that Dionne could get home before nightfall. I could almost hear the disapproval coming from Ms. Metcalfe.

Banishing the doubt, I gave Dionne's hand a squeeze. "One more try, and then we'll have to put it off until tomorrow. You need to eat something before you go."

She looked at me, face gray with the lack of energy. "I could stay... No, don't say it. I know, I have to go home." Her cheeks flushed with frustration. It made her look like she was about to collapse.

Torn between concern for her health and fear that if we stopped now, we'd never get a second chance, I tested the power flowing between us. It needed to be enough to complete a summoning. If we lost energy in the middle, it might cost us the solution. Ancients were hard to call once. If we lost one during the summoning, it might never return. I let go of her hand, because I couldn't be sure. It couldn't come to the point where I had to choose between the two apprentices. There was really no choice. Lionel would never forgive me if I let anything happen to Dionne. She was young enough to forgive me, eventually. "Let's restart tomorrow."

She slumped, and I realized she'd been pushing too much of her power into the spells and into the appearance of being stronger than she was. I felt the familiar disappointment in myself weigh on me. In the time we'd been together, I'd forgotten to teach her about managing her power. It was so strong that we'd never gotten to this state before, but that was no excuse. It was a basic lesson that all wizards learned.

There was still time to strengthen her energy before I sent her home. "Clear the circle and pull in any residual power. I'll go make us some dinner."

"No, I can do one more spell," she pleaded. "Don't worry about me. I'm young, I'll get the energy back fast."

I reached to pull her to her feet. She swayed in exhaustion when she was standing. Glad that I had resisted the urge to try one more summoning, I said, "There's time. We have all day tomorrow. Maybe after we've rested, we'll come up with a new idea."

I stirred the pot of stew. Lionel had shown me the benefit of having a pot of leftover food ready. She needed hearty food to rebuild herself. We didn't have enough time for me to teach her what she needed.

I knew that I was stuck with a hard choice. Dionne needed training and I was being too cautious. I could let her training fall behind, or I could let her take my books home. If anyone found the books on Dionne, they would ask too many questions. We couldn't afford the attention at any time, let alone now. None of the books were completely benign, all of them had spells that needed some kind of ingredient like mummified bats, or widow's tears. I was still anxiously trying to think through the options when she plodded across the floor to join me at the stove.

"What did you mean? Pull in the residual power." Her voice was barely above a whisper.

Guilt replaced my anxiety as I realized that I'd overestimated her power level again. And I'd forgotten that she didn't know how to replenish energy from a circle right after I'd thought of it.

"Sit." I ladled a bowlful of stew for her, making sure it was mostly meat. The only way she would get enough energy back to get past her foster parents' scrutiny. "You gave too much to the spell. When you get home, go to bed and sleep. I don't want you collapsing tomorrow."

She dug into the bowl and started eating. "Okay. I don't think that will be hard," she said with her mouthful. "Are we going to do the rest of this spell tomorrow?"

I made the decision. I was being too cautious. Dionne knew how to keep secrets. I was going to have to trust her. "We are, but I need you to learn something before you come back. This is something that can't be seen by your foster parents, or your friends." I waited until she'd agreed and then left her eating the stew to retrieve my spell primer. By the time I returned, she was looking a little less like she was on death's door. Relieved, I placed the book on the counter next to her.

"Okay, there are four spells here. I've marked them. They will teach you how to conserve your strength so that you can continue to do spells over the long haul. Only learn these four. And get your rest first, don't even crack the book until morning." I tried to make my words a command, but it sounded more like a plea.

"Okay, I promise." She looked at me and I must have looked surprised. "What? I promise. I'll sleep first. I won't let anyone else see the book, and I will only look at the spells you marked. Even though I think I should be able to look at all of them. This is like a kid's book, right?"

I felt the tug of her apprentice oath. She meant what she was saying. Too bad she hadn't been able to resist the last part. I couldn't lie to her, it was a primer after all. Trying to put enthusiasm into my voice, I said, "It is. And you'll probably learn the spells quickly. I promise that you will have a chance to go through all the spells in the book. Some of them have to be practiced here, but you will get your training. I'm sorry I didn't think to do this earlier."

"We had other things on our mind," she said. "Besides, Lionel was teaching me. If he hadn't... well, you know."

I was touched at her attempt to let me off the hook. "I let Lionel take too much responsibility. He's an apprentice, and he thinks like one."

She glared at me. "Hey, he did the best he could. It's not like we had a lot of spare time."

I liked her defense of him. "I didn't mean he did anything wrong," I said. "An apprentice thinks about getting as much knowledge as possible in a short time. That's what they should think about. As a teacher, I think about building up the knowledge from the basics. Lionel just forgot that you hadn't learned the basics from the time you could talk."

"Fine, but we are going to keep working until we fix what I did?" she asked, eyes still on the book.

I wanted to tell her yes, but I couldn't. I was too tired to argue, so I reluctantly compromised. Balancing between the absolute truth and the lie I wanted to say, I answered, "As long as we can, but the prophecy is going to become more important really soon."

I saw the knowledge in her eyes. I hadn't needed to tell her; Dionne knew that Lionel was less important in the bigger scheme of things. "But not yet, right?"

I nodded and pushed the primer toward her. She touched the book rubbing her fingers across the leather, clearly starving for the knowledge as much as she had been for the food. I ate my serving of stew as I walked her through the first spell.

5

We were cleaning the dishes when someone banged on my door.

"I'll get it," Dionne said. She ran to the door before I could stop her. Although I'm not sure why I wanted to. Maybe The Morrigan's warning had alerted me to possible threats.

I heard her say something inviting, and then footsteps approached. I moved away from the sink to position myself between the kitchen and the basement door. If this was someone coming to attack, I was going to keep them from Lionel.

A stranger followed Dionne into the room. He was about my height, but more heavily muscled. His brown hair was a little long, and mashed on his head like he'd been wearing a hat. He had dark green eyes that stared back at me with no concern. He was wearing a set of biking leathers, which might explain the hair. I saw a black tattoo peeking from the collar of his jacket. There was power emanating from him, but I had no idea what type of Real Folk he was.

"Welcome to my home," I said. "You have permission to stay if you bring no harm."

He smiled broadly. "Harm is a vague notion. I promise not to do purposeful damage, will that do?"

Since no one had come up with a foolproof ward that allowed people to move around and converse, it would have to do. "Who are you?"

"My name is Trahaearn. I'm the arch druid for this part of the world."

I didn't feel that druid vibe from him. He wasn't wearing robes, he was alone, and he didn't speak in whispers. "I've never heard of you."

He coughed, a dry sound like dust in his throat. "I just rose to arch druid. We lost our last leader to the southern continent. They needed someone experienced. He wanted to make a change."

Dionne fidgeted. "Perhaps our guest would like some water?"

I glanced at Trahaearn and he nodded. While Dionne filled a glass, I asked him, "Why are you here?"

He took the glass from Dionne and drank deeply before answering. As he swallowed, I saw his tattoo pulse. Wiping his mouth, he answered," I was called here by pain."

"What do you want of me?" I hoped it was something quick, but the way my life was going, I doubted it.

"I don't know. I came here and found Banks'. The bartender said I should talk to you if there was a problem with the druids." He grimaced, clearly not wanting to be in my debt.

I wasn't convinced he was a druid. I didn't know what he'd told Mark, but I trusted the troll to be careful with giving my name, so it must have been something verifiable. "I've had some dealing with the local druids."

"That's part of my problem." His face tightened with a flash of what must be the pain he felt. "I don't know where the local druids congregate."

That was odd. Unless the arch druid was very different from

other Real Folk, he should be able to tune into his people and find them without help. "Shouldn't you be able to sense them?"

I watched his reaction, my resentment forgotten in my fascination. Trahaearn rubbed his arm and his already pale skin became almost translucent in contrast to the tattoo. "I can feel the pain more now that I am closer, but I cannot sense any druids."

Dionne refreshed his water, sliding me a look that declared her desire to ask questions. I gave my head a shake. She could practice obedience. It could do double duty; teach her to obey and rebuild my trust in her oath, and her.

"Could they be blocking you?" I tried to think of reasons for the druids to avoid their leader, but nothing came to mind.

"No. A single druid can block me from their private thoughts, but not from the grove. Even if they all agreed to block me, I should feel the power from the grove through the earth. Even so, I do not believe a grove of druids would be able to bring consensus of all the members to block me."

I felt like I'd been shoved into a different world. If Trahaearn was the arch druid, and I still doubted him, then why would the druids block him? They seemed too bound by tradition for rebellion. "I think we need to test your assumptions."

He straightened and met my eyes with a glare. "Why do you wish to test me?" Well, at least, he had that druid attitude. He hated to be questioned.

Cautiously, I tested his patience with a bit more resistance. "I do not want to send you to the druids without knowing you have legitimate business there. I don't know you, and you have admitted that you can't connect to the local grove. I have never met a druid like you, but I know that if I create enemies of the druids, my life will be more difficult than it currently is. And that is going a long way."

He glanced at Dionne. "I am not used to being questioned in front of apprentices, no matter how pretty, or how powerful."

Dionne's eyes widened and she looked at me with fear. I knew it was fear of being left out, and I was not going to send her away. This lesson was something I couldn't make up. Learning to trust her feelings while leaving her options open was important to any apprentice. To Dionne it was vital. "She will stay until I send her away. My apprentice is not yours to instruct."

He shrugged, as though it was of no consequence, but I saw the tightening of his face that could have been anger, or defeat. "Very well. I sense your workspace in the basement. Is the floor open to the earth?"

"Yes, do you propose to cast a spell?" I would have to cast a disguise spell on Lionel. Or Dionne could do that if I sent her down first.

"I need to connect to the earth to access my power. I can do so in your backyard, but I think your neighbors will be suspicious of magical activity." He raised an eyebrow quizzically, and it felt like I should know more about druid magic than I did.

Resigned to the fact that he was going to the basement, I said, "I'll have my apprentice prepare the room." He didn't need to know what preparations needed to be made. I turned to Dionne. "Clear the circle, tidy the books, and spell evidence. And hide our most valuable fixture." I mouthed the words *disguise Lionel,* but she looked at me like I was telling her the sky was blue.

Dionne hurried downstairs as I turned back to Trahaearn. "I will allow you to use the space of my workroom. You will not conduct any spells that will harm me, or anyone in this house. You will leave the circle pure when you are finished." That should restrict him to just finding the local druids.

"I agree. I wish you no harm in any case." Trahaearn placed his glass on the counter. "I'm not immune to the threefold rule."

Dionne returned and smiled at both of us. "The room is ready, Quinn."

I led the way to the workroom so I could see the results of Dionne's quick clean up. I didn't care that much about the books or ingredients. The most important thing was Lionel's body, and the evidence of any work we'd done in the last couple of days. I stopped at the foot of the stairs and glanced at the couch under the window. If I didn't know that Lionel lay under the blanket, I would think there was just a pile of books. I don't know what had inspired her, but using the books to disguise his body rather than magic was an excellent idea.

The air was fresh, which meant she'd cleared the evidence of our magical searching. "Good work, Dionne." I walked to the center of the circle. "Trahaearn, what do you need for preparation?"

He glanced around. "Nothing. What do you need to allow you to trust me?"

I hadn't thought that far in advance. "Let's start with you trying to locate the grove without me. If you can do that then I'll believe you. If not, we'll figure something out." I wondered if the Drell museum qualified as the grove, or if there was a real grove somewhere. Some ancient circle of trees that fed the druid spells.

"That seems reasonable." Trahaearn shucked his jacket and laid it on the workbench we used to gather ingredients. He removed his black tee-shirt to reveal pale skin with an intricate tattoo running down the left side of his wiry body, black ink curving and twining into knots and patterns. Next, he removed his boots and socks, the tattoo must have covered the whole side of his body because there were tendrils of black ink that slithered under the sole of his left foot.

He knelt and placed his forehead on the ground. I saw his lips move, but there was no sound. I guessed he was calling to the earth. When he was done, he stood and lowered his hands to his side. Closing his eyes, Trahaearn let his body relax and I could feel his power touch the soil of my workspace. I watched Dionne as she focused on Trahaearn's magic. Her eyes traveled down his body to the ground and I could almost hear her questions bubbling up.

Trahaearn stood that way for at least ten minutes, and then knelt quickly and repeated his silent words to the soil. "I cannot feel anything. It is time to come up with another plan. Perhaps the spirit you summon regularly can assist."

It was time to get more answers. There was no way that I would be opening a circle here until I knew a lot more about this stranger. An apprentice came in handy when you didn't want to show your ignorance, but needed information. "Before we do anything more, I think it would be useful to instruct my apprentice in druid ways." I beckoned to Dionne. "Ask your questions."

Trahaearn slid his feet into his shoes as he answered. "Is this necessary? I feel an urgency to the pain."

Dionne raised an eyebrow and I just nodded. He was in our home, and he would do as I asked, no matter his standing among the druids. "We'll keep it short. But, yes, it is necessary."

He pulled his shirt over his head and looked at Dionne. Impatience vibrating off him, warring with his need to be polite. Definitely not our kind of druid. "Very well, but if you can't help me, I need to find someone who can. Perhaps someone in that vast park."

Dionne gestured for him to sit on the bench seat. "I only have a few questions. You must forgive my ignorance, I have only recently become an apprentice, but I thought druids were teachers."

He flushed at that, though her tone was respectful. "Yes, that is true. If this pain that calls me was not so insistent, I would be happy to spend time with you."

Dionne smiled and said, "I understand. So, if you can feel this pain, why can't you find the source?"

"It is not directional now that I am here. Have you ever experienced a toothache?"

Dionne nodded.

"Then you will understand what I feel. It is like that, when you are not sure which tooth is actually causing the pain. In California I knew the direction was north, and the intensity increased as I approached Vancouver."

"Okay, I can understand that. When you were using our soil, what exactly were you looking for?"

I thought that was a great question. If he hadn't found the energy from the museum, he couldn't have been looking for that.

"I was searching for the power we leave in the earth when we do magic. There should be a circle of clean power in the area. When I couldn't find that, I searched for strong trees, but your park is so well tended by the sprites that there are hundreds. I couldn't find a trace of the druid energy I expected."

I was surprised that he didn't take the opportunity to convince us that he was the arch druid. He seemed content to simply instruct Dionne. I was happy to let her keep asking questions. "What about a place of learning? Would you find druids there?"

Trahaearn rubbed his hands over his face. I could see the lines of weariness around his eyes when his hands returned to his lap. I guess a constant pain can be hard on the spirit. If the druids in the amulet were the cause, maybe he could help Lionel. That was if he could convince me he really was a druid, or maybe that he wouldn't make things worse.

He shrugged. "I felt nothing orderly enough to be druid work."

Dionne looked at me. I had no help for her. "Quinn, I think we should try a circle."

She was right. I would have to contain Trahaearn's magic and that would be a challenge, but we needed to resolve this. If he was a druid, he could hold the solution to our problems. And maybe there was some way for me to verify his identity.

Suddenly hopeful, I waved her to the stairs. "Okay, get the candy and I'll start things here."

When Dionne was upstairs, I asked Trahaearn, "How do I keep you from messing with the summoning?"

He laughed. "You don't trust that I am who I claim, yet you will trust me to give you constraints?"

It seemed he was less inclined to be polite to me. I pretended that he'd been less snide and said, "No, I will require your oath."

He glanced at Dionne as she reentered the room. "I will give you my oath if you will explain why you are teaching one of the six, and why you have a body under that blanket."

Dionne dropped the bowl of candy.

I ignored the noise. "The six need to be trained as much as anyone. I would appreciate you keeping Dionne's identity to yourself. There are political considerations that make it important she be kept secret until she is trained." I would find out later how he knew.

He seemed to consider. "I agree. And the body?"

So, he had infiltrated the disguise. "I will not discuss that."

"And I will not trade with someone who uses the magic of death."

"Quinn isn't using death magic," Dionne blurted out. "He would never do that."

I held up a hand to stop her telling Trahaearn the whole story. "We will not discuss it, but I give you my oath that I do not use the souls of other beings to power my magic."

He focused his gaze on mine. I controlled my impulse to defend myself as his green eyes seemed to drill into my brain. If he was the arch druid, I needed to keep him on my good side. I kept my gaze even, and waited for him to speak.

"Very well, we will exchange oaths. Perhaps when we have more trust, you will tell me the story of this body."

The oaths exchanged, it was time to set the circle and see if we could find some information on the grove. In the circle, I might also be able to sense Trahaearn's purpose, or otherwise get confirmation that he was a druid. With that, I would tell him where the museum was and send him on his way. Without it, I wasn't going to chance the ire of the druids I know.

"Dionne, set the circle. Trahaearn, stand beside me so we don't get in her way." I pointed to the center of the dirt floor.

We stood quietly watching Dionne draw a ring of salt around us. Trahaearn paid close attention to her technique. "She is well trained, Quinn. Does she use earth magic to set the circle for any particular reason?"

"I don't know. When she learned, I was blind, so my other apprentice taught her."

He shifted his interest to me. "Blind?"

"Long story." Maybe I would tell him another time, but right now I refused to be distracted.

Dionne finished the circle and motioned for us to sit. "How do you want to proceed?" she asked Trahaearn.

"It doesn't matter. Call your favorite spirit, and we'll see if it can help."

Dionne looked to me. "Call Ranseed." I figured we would start at the top. He wasn't the most friendly, but he would know what was going on if anything was.

"Ranseed, come at my calling, we have questions." Dionne threw the candy onto the ground and we waited. It didn't take long before the candy started to dance as if there was a whirlwind in the center of my basement.

"What do you want to know this time, wizard? I have already told you I cannot help with Lionel one name. And I do not wish to be tricked again."

"Keep your comments to yourself," Dionne said. "We have a guest."

"Fine," Ranseed answered. "What do I have to do for these paltry sweets?"

Dionne looked at Trahaearn. "Do you want to ask your question?"

He nodded and touched the earth with his bare hand. As soon as his skin made contact, his power crept to find us. There was no threat, only a touch, as if he needed to make contact with every-thing around him.

Trahaearn fixed his gaze about six inches above the earth, as if he could see Ranseed. "Do you know me?"

Ranseed laughed. I wondered what experience Trahaearn had with the spirits. There weren't enough candies in the circle, if Ranseed wanted payment for every question.

Apparently Ranseed was in a chatty mood because he said, "I know what you are, druid."

That answered one of my concerns. Trahaearn kept his eyes fixed on the same place and asked, "Are there others like me here?"

There was a faint sound of leaves rustling. "That is a second question. What will you give me for the answer?"

Trahaearn reached into his pocket and pulled out a handful of chocolates, placing one on the ground. "One of these."

"Very good. No. There are no others like you here," Ranseed seemed to pause before he fell silent.

Trahaearn's eyes narrowed. I knew Ranseed well enough that I had no doubt he was withholding information. Trahaearn was suspicious, but I thought I would need to step in.

"Spirit, what else do you know?" The problem with Trahaearn's question was that he didn't make it specific enough.

"I know many things, druid. For instance, I know that the original purpose of the druid was to teach. It seems that you have more to learn than you have to teach."

Trahaearn closed his eyes and muttered something I couldn't hear. I would have put money on it that he was berating himself for the slip.

"What do you know that is germane to my question?" Much better, I'd have to remember that the next time we asked for information.

"There are no chocolates on the ground," Ranseed said.

Trahaearn took another chocolate and placed it on the ground before asking the question again.

Ranseed made the treat dance on the dirt. "There are those who claim to be the same as you living within this city. There are some like you, but they are not here." Knowing about the amulet, I thought the meaning of his last word was clear. He wasn't finished. "And there are those who are neither here nor like you." The chocolate disappeared. "Do you have other questions?"

Trahaearn removed his hand from the dirt. "Not at this time. Perhaps the others do."

I told Dionne to finish the session. She dismissed Ranseed and started to clear the circle when there was a shriek of wind and a cry of pain from the earth.

"Stop, stop, stop. Don't let it continue, release..."

Trahaearn reached for the earth. "What has happened here?"

The sound of the wind died, and the feeling of desolation lifted.

Dionne stared at the ground. "What did I do wrong?"

I cleared the energy from the circle and wiped a break in the salt ring. "Nothing. We need to do a cleansing again."

Trahaearn grabbed my arm. "Does this happen all the time?"

I'd felt enough of his power to trust that he wasn't out to harm anyone, and Ranseed had confirmed that he was a druid, so I decided to trust him. "No. It started around the time Dionne arrived, and I think it has something to do with the prophecy."

He looked at Dionne before answering. "No, it had nothing to do with the prophecy. Or, rather, it has nothing to do with your apprentice. That was the voice of a tortured spirit. A tortured druid spirit."

The amulet. Perhaps this was something to do with Lionel. "I think it's time we talked."

6

When we got back upstairs, I noticed it was getting dark. "Dionne, you need to go home now."

"But, Quinn..."

I was not in the mood to be cajoled. Ms. Metcalfe's suspicion had scared me. It would help to have her gone while Trahaearn and I talked about the prophecy and Lionel. I wasn't sure what he knew, and I wanted time to process it into a lesson rather than let her jump to conclusions. Ones I bet would be risky and bring the attention of the government.

"Dionne, go home. You can come back tomorrow. I promise nothing important will happen until then." I waited until she nodded, and then said, "Tomorrow will be a more successful day. I feel it in my bones."

She rolled her eyes. "Yeah, I hope so too. Goodnight, Quinn. Goodnight, Trahaearn."

He gave a small bow. "Sleep well, apprentice."

"Fine. Don't forget to eat something. I'll be back as early as I can."

We waited for her to go, and then I dug around in the kitchen for something to make into a meal for my guest. There was cheese, and bread, and apples, it would have to do. "It's a bit sparse, my other apprentice usually does the grocery shopping. I assume you would rather not go to Banks' at this time. It will be busy and everyone will want to get to know you."

He cleared space at the counter. "Yes, I think it would make sense to keep a low profile until we work out what's going on. Can I help?"

I waved him to sit. "Since I got my sight back, I like to do everything for myself." I sliced bread and cheese for the plate. I pulled a couple of beers from the fridge.

He reached for the bottles and the tops popped off. "I would prevail upon your hospitality for the night. I need to find the source of the pain I feel, but I think a night's rest will be of more help than wandering the streets looking for something that is reputedly not there."

I'd expected him to ask for assistance, maybe introductions in the park to help in finding this grove. I was happy to put him up for the night since we needed to talk about what happened, but there was no way I was going to let him sleep in Lionel's room. "You can sleep on the couch up here." I pointed. "It's comfortable."

Trahaearn took a long drink of the beer. "Thanks. I like sleeping on the ground occasionally, but it's been too long since I had a soft surface under me at night."

I picked at the plate of food I had in front of me. Trahaearn wolfed his sandwich down. I wanted to start the conversation, but I wasn't sure where. The fact that I knew about the druids was going to sound like I'd been lying earlier. Lionel's body and the Gur amulet were only going to make it sound worse. But it all needed to be on the table, and waiting wasn't going to make it easier.

Trahaearn broke the silence. "I think that we've both been dancing around information because we have no trust."

"True."

"Do we have trust now?" Trahaearn asked, tipping the bottle to see if there was more beer.

I retrieved two more bottles. "I can only speak for myself. I trust you. If there was any reason not to, Ranseed would have said something."

"The spirit always warns you of danger? I wish I had such reliable assistance from that world."

"No, but he likes Lionel for some reason. If you were a danger, he would have let us know."

"Well, wizard, I have always lived my life trusting others until given reason not to. So, we seem to have trust."

It was time to come clean. I wasn't going to just throw information at him, though. "I have a deal to discuss."

He leaned his elbows on the counter. "A deal? What is it that you could possibly offer other than information?"

"I will give you the information. I am offering help for help. You will need my help dealing with the source of your pain, if I am right. And I think you can help me with at least one of my current problems."

He frowned. I hope it was in thinking it over, rather than concentrating on how he could get the information without the deal. "If there are no druids in the area, how will you help? If I don't have all the information, how will I know the value of the bargain?"

"I know what Ranseed meant by his answer. If we have a deal, I will explain everything. If not, I can give you the information on where to find the local grove. Believe me, you will want the help along with the information."

"I do not enter into bargains lightly. I rarely do it without knowing the full scope of the deal, and I never do it when I am tired. Will you give me until the morning to decide?"

It seemed reasonable. In fact, it was more than I would get from the local druids who would have pressured me for an answer. "Fine."

"So, the information?"

Taking the final two bottles of beer from the fridge, I let Trahaearn do his cap popping trick and settled in. "I'm not sure how far back to go."

"We have all night, so start at the beginning."

That wouldn't work. There were too many beginnings to this story. "The beginning depends on your belief system. Perhaps I'll start with Fionuir."

Over the next couple of hours, I explained what had gone on in as much detail as I could. Trahaearn asked few questions during my tale, which let me manage the order of the facts. "Then Lionel ended up in the amulet. I don't know how long his body will survive without his spirit, but we're doing everything we can to reunite them."

"This is the first of your current problems. What is the other?"

"The prophecy of the six. I am trying to find out how to prepare Dionne for what is coming."

He nodded, and I saw the weariness in his movement. "It must be a burden to train the bringer of such change."

A little shower of hope filled me. "So, you know what the prophecy is about?"

"Nice try." He chuckled. "I will sleep on it, but I think our bargain needs to be that I will help you with both of your problems, and you will assist me with mine."

It sounded like I was going to get the best of that deal. I knew that it wouldn't be true, but if he could bring Lionel back and help with the prophecy, I would happily pay his price, no matter what it was that I was missing in his offer. "I'll leave you to your thinking. Let me get you a blanket and pillow."

❧ 7 ❧

The next morning, I rose to the sound of Dionne announcing her entrance. It was barely light. Looking out my window, I saw Trahaearn rise from the garden, brushing his knees, and muttering something I couldn't hear. I guess he needed to deal with some druid stuff. Doing it before dawn was the best way to avoid notice.

I brushed my teeth and gabbed clothes, pulling them on to the sound of Dionne talking to Trahaearn. "I'm sorry I slept in. I didn't expect you this early, Dionne," I said as I closed my door behind me.

"It's Sunday. I've done my homework, and my chores. I can get breakfast while you tell me what happened last night." She started opening cupboards without waiting for me to answer. "Man, I need to go shopping for you. Give me the credit card, or some cash, and I'll get supplies tomorrow before I come over."

Trahaearn looked at me with a stupid grin on his face. "I am beginning to wonder who is the apprentice and who the master."

"Any advice you have on the subject is welcome." I laughed at Dionne's reaction. "You are bossy and you know it. That's probably why you can bend the apprentice oath. Thanks for offering to shop. I'll give you some cash later. Now we need to talk."

She rolled her eyes and turned to make oatmeal. "What happened last night?"

"Nothing. I told Trahaearn about everything that has happened since Fionuir tried to keep her power." I took the tea she offered.

"Everything?" She didn't look at us. "Even what I did."

I hadn't wanted her to know she'd killed Cate when she tried to call her parent's souls from death. It seems she found out somehow. I guess I couldn't expect everyone to keep it secret. "Everything that he needed to know."

Trahaearn put his mug down on the counter. "I thought we had no secrets. If you have not been fully open with me, I don't know if I can consider a deal."

Before I could say it wasn't about our deal, Dionne spoke, "I killed Cate. It wasn't on purpose. I was trying to contact my parents before I knew what I was, and I accidentally summoned a demon that killed her." I heard all the pain I felt at Cate's loss in her voice. The difference was her pain was tainted with guilt, and mine was starting to heal.

I made her look at me before saying, "Dionne, it's okay. You don't need to feel at fault."

Trahaearn waved a hand to stop her speaking. "You think you are going to make a mistake at a critical point. I sense you feel responsible for Lionel's condition. You know that we all make mistakes when we are learning?"

She sobbed a breath. "I split his spirit from his body. Of course, I am responsible."

"No," I said. "You saved his life."

Tears were falling from her eyelashes. "No. Until we get him back together, I haven't saved his life."

I wanted to argue, but Trahaearn intercepted my comments. "You did the right thing, Dionne. I know that you feel like you could have done better, but I might not have had the presence of mind to throw two spells at once." He went to the stove to stir the forgotten pot of oatmeal. "You are afraid that you'll mess up the prophecy of the six because you haven't trained long enough."

She wiped her eyes and glared at his back. "Are you some kind of psychic?"

I needed to take control. "Dionne, don't be rude."

Trahaearn reached for the bowls she'd placed on the counter. "No, I'm not a mind reader. I've been in your place. Perhaps I'll tell the story after we've done our business."

She perked up. "Does that mean you'll help?"

I motioned for her to sit at the counter. "Dionne, please don't pressure our guest." I waited for the druid to put his food on the counter before doing exactly that. "You've done your thinking?"

He nodded and dug the spoon into his breakfast. "I think my problem is going to prove more complicated than I expected. So, we need to formalize the deal."

Now we were on familiar druid territory. "What do you mean, formalize?" I hoped Dionne knew to keep her mouth closed at this point in the negotiations.

"It seems to me that I need you to help with this pain I sense. I said that I would help you with both Lionel and the prophecy. This morning I used your garden to get advice from my own earth spirits. They tell me that our deal is an even trade despite appearances."

Now I was the one jealous of his contacts. I never got real advice from my contacts in the spirit world. "I imagine that the prophecy will have an effect on all Real Folk. Did your spirit have any other information?"

He smiled. "No, my spirit continues to advise me that there are no druids living in this area. Perhaps I am not asking the right questions."

It worried me that I seemed to be the only person who knew the local druids, but it was good leverage. "Okay so the deal is this. First you help us put Lionel back together, and then we deal with the prophecy, and then with your problem."

Trahaearn roared a laugh. "Very nice try, wizard. No, I think we will do this in a different order. Bringing his spirit back to your apprentice means we will have another hand in helping to solve my problem, so that will be done first. And then, when my problem is solved, we will prepare for the prophecy."

It seemed more fair. It also seemed too easy. "What if the prophecy has a different deadline?"

"Then we will deal with it on its time line. In fact, that is half of the problem, right? The prophecy rules over our wishes." He reached out a hand. "Let us shake on it. We will follow our schedule, Lionel, my problem, the prophecy. If the control is wrested from us, we will follow fate."

I shook hands. "Done. Now, I think Dionne is about to burst with questions."

The words fell from her as though someone had broken the bottle she'd captured them in. "How long will we wait until Lionel is back with us? What do you know about the prophecy? No one else has any information, and we've asked everyone."

He pushed his bowl toward her. "While you are cleaning the dishes, I will answer your questions." He waited until she had filled the sink with soapy water. "Now, as to the first question, we will have Lionel back today. And to the second, I don't have much information, but I hope we will have access to more knowledge when we have found the source of the pain and resolved it."

※ 8 ※

Trahaearn knelt before Lionel's body, reaching delicately to touch his skin, or as close as he could get to it through the spell. "He is warm. His body still functions without the spirit."

"Can you touch him? I feel a barrier." Was it just me?

Trahaearn shook his head. "It is not a barrier. It is a difference in the passage of time. You are touching him, no matter what your mind tells you."

I didn't say anything. There really was nothing to say. The fact was we didn't know how the spell worked. If Lionel's body was slowed down enough, he could still be dying. It would be a long process, maybe eons, but still dying. If he was preserved, then when we restored him, there would be no change, at least physically.

"We need to have him in the circle with us." Trahaearn pulled the blanket off and picked Lionel up in one swift move. "I think he'll need to touch the ground, so make the circle wide."

I tried not to worry at the fact he seemed unsure, although his words didn't match his attitude. He acted like we were his students. I know I shouldn't let it bother me, but it rankled.

This was my workshop. He could at least stop acting like it was his.

Dionne hefted the salt bag that she'd pulled from the back of the workbench at his command. "We're low. I'll go up and get what we have in the kitchen." She trotted up the stairs.

I helped to arrange Lionel on the ground. We placed him face down and pressed his palms to the soil. "His spirit will be able to reenter his body through those points." Trahaearn placed the blanket across Lionel. I tucked it in as best I could.

Dionne clattered down the stairs with a full bag of salt in her arms. "Okay, what do we need to do now?"

It was odd to let someone else take over in my workspace, but I tried to push aside the possessive urges, telling myself I was an observer, not a student.

Trahaearn gestured for her to create a circle around us. "We need to know as much as we can about the place we are entering." He looked to me.

I watched Dionne cast the salt, making sure she paid attention to the spell, and not our preparations. I wasn't going to let her get into a situation where she piled more guilt on herself. "All we know is that there are druid souls inside. They were placed there to keep them safe when their bodies were murdered."

Trahaearn slipped out of his boots and sat next to Lionel. "Have you seen the amulet?"

Dionne finished the circle and placed the sack of salt of the floor just inside the ring. She sat at Lionel's head, facing Trahaearn. I moved to sit at his side, forming a triangle of our bodies. "We had it in our possession for a short period," I said. "It's nothing special. A stone with markings and bands of metal."

"Dionne, place your right hand on Lionel's head and hold Quinn's right hand in your left." Trahaearn waited for us to obey. "Now take my right hand, Quinn. Don't let go until we are done." He placed his left hand on Lionel's bare ankle

We hadn't answered his question, but now we were linked in a circle to mirror the salt protecting us. I could feel warmth flowing across my body from Trahaearn's power.

He muttered a few words, but they made no sense to me. When it stopped, it felt like my hands were fused to Dionne and Trahaearn's. He said, "It will be difficult, but not impossible to break our bond. When we enter the amulet, we must stay linked in this world to ensure we can leave. The only reason to break it is a mortal threat. Do not attempt it otherwise."

I turned to Dionne. "Are you going to follow the instructions? No testing your oath this time. I don't want you lost in there."

"Okay," Dionne said. "Um... how will we know it's a mortal threat? Not, just something real bad."

He chuckled. "A good question. I think you will know. Our bodies will be here, our souls will enter the amulet. If our hands separate, Quinn is right, there is danger that our souls will be added to the number trapped inside."

"Dionne, just don't let go unless one of us tells you to." I wasn't sure that I would recognize a mortal threat, but I was less likely to be frightened by the unusual than Dionne.

"Now, I need you to visualize the amulet," Trahaearn said. "When you have it in your mind, I will locate the interior. Then we will enter."

Dionne jerked her hand but didn't let go. "Wait, you are going to be in my head?"

"Not inside, just at the edge," he assured her. "I will see what you are thinking about, so focus on the amulet. Your secrets are safe, unless you think about them."

"Okay, just make sure you don't get in my head." She squeezed my hand. "Let's do this."

"Visualize the amulet." Trahaearn's words were quiet, but they echoed in my mind more than my ears.

I thought about the last time I'd seen it. The amulet wasn't that large, mostly it was gray stone with a few bands of bronze.

"Good," Trahaearn said. "I know this type of amulet. It's

ancient but stable. I know how we can enter. We need to prepare. Relax until we are ready. We may be there for a long time." Trahaearn didn't take us into the amulet, he started talking as though passing time. "I don't know who placed the souls in there. It is not a place to hold anything that thinks or feels. I do not know what we will encounter."

I was pretty sure we wouldn't be encountering anything sweet. "We'll be prepared."

"And what about Dionne? Will you risk the prophecy?" His words rang with an anxious energy. It was as if he'd had a vision.

I started to ask if he had more than just concern, but Dionne cut my words off.

"There is no way I am staying here. I sent Lionel there. I have to get him out." Guilt laced her words. I knew that she would not feel released from that until he was whole and able to forgive her.

Trahaearn looked at me. "Will you risk her?"

I realized that I hadn't thought of it as risking Dionne. He was right. If something happened to her, aside from how I would feel, which made me sick to even think about, the prophecy would be stopped. But I didn't control her. I taught her when we weren't running from one disaster or another, but she was her own person. Even as a teenager, her life was hers to risk.

"Dionne, the prophecy needs to happen."

"No," she said. "It will happen if the time is right. You know that, Quinn. If it will happen, I will survive until it does. So, I'm going."

"And you promise to do as Trahaearn asks?" It bothered me to keep asking that question. If she hadn't been so quick to do as she wanted, regardless of anyone's wishes, I would not have asked it even once.

"Yes, I already said I would," she answered. "I'll keep holding hands until someone tells me to let go, or we are back here."

There wasn't much I could do to argue with her. We needed to get this done. I wouldn't feel good about this until we had Lionel back. I told Trahaearn, "I agree with Dionne. She needs to be part of this. There will be lessons in this that I cannot teach her any other way."

Trahaearn glanced between us and then to Lionel's body. After a few moments, he nodded. "Very well. Remember what I said. Do not let go of the link until we are back here." He motioned for us to get comfortable again, and then whispered, "Ready?"

He didn't wait for our answer because we were whirling through the earth as if it were air before I could form the words. Our movement slowed, and we found ourselves standing in a long corridor. The walls were translucent, and out of the corner of my eyes I caught swift movements. It was disorienting when I turned my attention to the motion and found nothing there.

"The amulet," Trahaearn's voice appeared in my mind as sounds and written words.

"Don't try to speak," his voice told me. "Just watch."

I obeyed the command, although I'm not sure I could have disobeyed it if I wanted to. I could see Dionne as a shadow on the other side of Trahaearn. Her lips were moving, but I couldn't hear what she was saying. What I could feel was her hand in mine, despite the sight of her walking beside the druid.

Soft shrieks called to us as we started to move. It was as though I was shielded from terror, but also feeling it pass through me. Similar to that sudden flash of goose bumps when something evil crosses your grave. If I wasn't holding onto Dionne and Trahaearn, I'm not sure I would have been able to negotiate my way through the maze of the amulet.

As we moved, something would take my breath and then give it back, as though I was breathing with the amulet.

We traveled the length of the corridor and turned the corner. The movements on the periphery of my vision, although I guess it was Trahaearn's vision really, continued. I also had a sense that he was hearing something we could not. He flinched a couple of times for no reason I could see.

I realized we were following some path through a maze. I told myself to remember to ask Trahaearn about this when we were done. We reached the center where a glow of amber light shone, making the walls look like onionskins.

Trahaearn squeezed my hand before calling out. "Lionel, if you are here come to the core."

We waited.

The movements came more into focus and formed shapes. I saw eyes and noses in wisps of vapor. The trapped souls were gathering. Voiceless screams somehow echoed in my mind like a memory of terror.

"Lionel, I am Trahaearn, arch druid of this realm and commander of the magic in this amulet. I demand you come to me."

I wished for the ability to talk, to reach out to Lionel, and convince him to come to us, but I feared that my voice would break the spell holding us in the amulet. If that happened, we might join these souls.

"He answers from far away. This amulet is folded upon itself. My power weakens as it goes out to the edges. He does not wish to place us in danger. He feels as though his presence is holding back a horror."

I waited for Trahaearn to give me permission to speak, or think. He needed something from me and I had no idea what it was.

"Is there something that we can say to allay his fears? If there is, think it and I will hear," he said.

I could only think of telling him we were safe, but I didn't know how to get him to believe it.

"Thank you, Dionne."

Trahaearn's voice came to me, and I hoped that Dionne had given him the right words. "Lionel, you are forgiven. It is safe to return. Dionne needs you for the prophecy. We beg you to return."

Nothing happened. I had no idea what Lionel might have done that needed forgiving. I was the one who let all this happen. I kept my focus on the hall ahead of me, doing my best to ignore the pain emanating from the souls around us.

"No!" Trahaearn's mental shout tore my gaze to his side. Dionne was gone. "Damn you, woman. You need to learn to heed your teachers."

I could feel her fingers in mine, but she was no longer with us. "Where is she?" I screamed at Trahaearn, no longer bound to his will.

"She ran. We heard Lionel refuse to come again. He said there was someone he needed to protect."

"I still have her hand."

"As do I. We must trust that is enough."

"Can we follow her? Can you see where she is?"

He squeezed my hand, it was reassuring. "I can sense where she is. If she does not return soon, we will go toward that location."

How would we know when to go? Time within this world didn't feel right. I couldn't tell if we had been here minutes or hours. Or days. "When will we go?"

Trahaearn looked around. "It has only been a few seconds since she went. There is something happening where they are. There is another spirit there."

I burned to go and help. "We need to be there."

"Quinn, we are safer here. She knows where we are. When we leave, it must be worth the risk of losing contact with them. I cannot guarantee that I will not get us lost in this world. We do not know how long it takes for us to become like these sad souls."

I didn't care. "My apprentices are both here. I have nothing of value outside this world."

He pulled me closer. "You owe me, wizard. You have that to return to, if nothing else."

It wasn't enough. "Can you still see them?"

"Yes. There is more, Quinn."

"What are you talking about? More? More what?"

"These souls. The ones around us are druids, but the one who is with Dionne and Lionel, it is not a druid. It is a sprite."

That wasn't possible. Myrddin had been very clear that they had saved the souls of their murdered brothers. There was no reason to place anyone else here. "Is that the only one who is not a druid?"

"As far as I can tell. I suspect that you have not been given the entire story, Quinn. There is a very thin line between sanctuary and prison."

"We'll deal with it when we have Dionne and Lionel back." There was no way I would protect Myrddin and his brothers from Trahaearn any longer. In the short time I had known him, this arch druid had acted more like a friend than any of the local druids. And I'd saved their asses with the amulet for less than a thank you. I'd done nothing for Trahaearn but promise to help.

9

"They are returning." Trahaearn's words broke my train of thought. "Two souls. One is Dionne, one Lionel."

Relief flooded me. Whatever Dionne had done to convince Lionel had worked, and we could leave this place. I would trust them to tell me when we were back in the, relatively sane, real world.

I saw them return. Dionne's spirit was bright and whole compared to the ones around us. Lionel's was still bright, but there were tattered edges starting to show. If it only took a few days to start the process of deterioration, how long had these others been here?

Relief calmed me as Dionne joined us again. "He's fine. Let's get out of here."

Trahaearn held us in place. "I will return you to your bodies, but I must ask that you hold my hands until I am back with you. There are questions here that I need answers to, and that means I will need to stay."

When his words ended, I found myself back in my body. Looking across I saw Dionne's spirit return like a light going on behind her eyes. One second the stare was blank, the next a gleam of joy shone at me. "Keep hold of Trahaearn," I reminded her.

Lionel groaned and started to turn over. "No, don't move," Dionne said. "You are part of the circle."

His head returned to the ground, cheek down. "How long?" His voice creaked from disuse.

"A few days," I said.

"Who came?" He coughed. "Who brought you there to find me?"

I told him what we knew about Trahaearn.

"Good, he will understand. I hope he returns soon, the ground is cold and damp. I thought the power would have come back by now."

"Understand what?" Dionne asked. "What happened in there? Who was that with you?"

Lionel cleared his throat again. "It was hard to know. He said he was one of Moss's people, but the Moss he described was only ten feet tall. Is it possible that one of them was taken that long ago?"

If the sprite was accurate, it would have been almost a hundred years. The only explanation I could come up with was that the sprite was caught in the spell when the druids were sent there. But I would have remembered if druids were murdered in such recent times. When Myrddin told us the tale of the druid souls, he'd indicated that it was centuries ago.

I'd assumed that it was around the time of the purge. Three hundred years ago. When the humans had annihilated the vampires. Human history had forgotten what happened, but I hadn't. If that were true, Moss would have been only five or six feet tall at that time.

Figuring time would pass easier if we talked, I asked, "Did this sprite mention whether the other souls were there before it came?"

"No, we didn't do much chatting, sorry. If I had known I was coming back, I would have gathered more information." He coughed again.

I hoped that Trahaearn's questions were easy to answer. Every dry breath that Lionel took, broke something inside me. "Rest, we'll wait for Trahaearn in quiet. Perhaps Dionne can meditate on her understanding of a promise."

She looked at me eyes wide. "But if I hadn't gone—"

I glared at her. She really didn't understand what had happened to me when she ran for Lionel. "I'm not saying you shouldn't have gone. I'm saying you should have at least told us, and at best, asked us if you could go."

I could see the rebellion as if the word was tattooed on her forehead. But she deflated, hopefully realizing her mistake, and closed her eyes.

Of course, now that we were only waiting, I started to feel all those irritations that make me fidget. My nose itched simply because I couldn't scratch it. It felt like a bug was crawling up my pant leg, and my toe was cramping. I looked at Dionne, and she was twitching her nose, so it wasn't just me. "Okay, this can be a lesson in patience." It was true, but it also gave me something other than my own twitches to think about. I took a deep breath to clear my head of the distractions. "Everything that is trying to get you to drop the connection to Trahaearn can be ignored."

Dionne blew her hair out of her eyes. "Please, Quinn, don't keep us in suspense. I need to sneeze really badly and it's just going to have to be uncovered if you don't tell me how to stop it. What exactly is the lesson?"

"Lionel, what's the first step?"

He grunted. "First, try accepting the distraction. It might go away."

We gave that a few seconds. Okay, I'm not the most patient at this exercise. "The next step is to isolate it in a separate place in your mind." My own fidgets were fading as I watched Dionne concentrate on the lesson. After a minute of furrowing her brow and twisting her lips in frustration, it was clear she was losing the battle. "Okay, the last trick is to turn it into a contest. Imagine that this is a spell being thrown at you. Now your goal is to win against your foe."

Her eyes narrowed and then a grin brightened her face. "Hey, that worked."

"Yes, you are a fighter," Trahaearn said breaking the connection between us. "I apologize for keeping you in this position. We must discuss what I have learned and make a plan to act now."

As we made our way upstairs I noticed that Lionel moved better than I expected for someone who had basically been bedridden for almost a week. He was slower than usual, but not enough to show that his body had been inactive for several days. "We will get to our part of the bargain, Trahaearn. Can you give Lionel a chance to catch his breath?"

He glanced at Lionel as if seeing him for the first time. "I apologize, but my task has become more urgent. Of course, we can wait for your apprentice to recover. I will tell you what I have discovered while he eats."

Lionel gave a little cough, not the dry one, but one of those polite indications that he needs to speak. Usually he would simply talk if he had something to say. His time in the amulet must have taught him manners. Or perhaps, he was concerned about our guest. I nodded permission to continue.

"You don't need to wait for me. I can eat and listen."

Dionne set a bowl of reheated stew in front of Lionel. I hoped his system would be able to manage the richness, and be able to stay awake long enough to learn what he needed to know.

As he dug in, Dionne said, "I know I'm just an apprentice, but I think it might help if we heard Lionel's story first. And he needs to know what's been happening here."

Trahaearn took a stool. "You may be an apprentice, but there is no only about you. You are one of the six, and you are a very perceptive woman."

That made me chuckle. Perceptive, maybe. Headstrong, definitely. I pulled out a seat for her and went to attend the kettle. "Let's start with bringing Lionel up to date. I'm sure you agree that he will be more help if he is informed."

Trahaearn shrugged. "Of course. Let me tell him my story."

I shook my head. "I want Dionne to get used to passing on information without adding her editorial comments. It's a skill she needs to hone before she screws up a message, or worse, a spell."

I could see from the way Trahaearn's frown creased his face that he wasn't enjoying my role as the head of the household. I understood it. Being arch druid probably meant his word was law, but these were my apprentices and this was my home, and I was tired of feeling like I was imposing on him.

"Okay." Dionne tapped her chin. "Here's the scoop. Trahaearn is the arch druid, he's here because something painful is calling him."

I watched Trahaearn while she spoke. He leaned forward as if to interrupt when she mentioned the reason for his arrival, but he firmed his lips and kept quiet.

"Quinn made a deal, and the first part was getting you out of the amulet. Now we have to help him with his problem before he will give us what he knows about the prophecy." She glanced at me before continuing, "That's the basics. I don't know why he knew all about getting you home when you-know-who said there was no way."

Lionel glanced at Trahaearn. I wonder if something happened between them that we were blocked from seeing. Or, maybe, it was just a shared knowledge of the amulet world.

"I guess it's my turn." Lionel had barely dented the bowl of stew, but his color was improving, so I let it go. "At first, I couldn't understand what was happening. I heard moans and screams, but only saw vapor coalescing with the sound. I don't know how long I was in there. It felt like a lifetime." His gaze became distant.

After a moment, I realized he wasn't going to continue. Before I could prompt him, Trahaearn interrupted, "I know what that world is like, Lionel. Can you just tell us what you learned so we can continue? It will take years to resolve your feelings about it."

Lionel shuddered, and then focused on Trahaearn. "Thank you for shielding them from the worst of the pain. I think it's important to give an understanding of the reality there. I'm not sure that the things I learned will make sense otherwise."

Visibly stifling his impatience, Trahaearn waved his hand for Lionel to continue.

Lionel rubbed his face and then said, "Thank you. The longer I stayed, the more I was able to discern the other inhabitants. Perhaps I was becoming more like them. Anyway, I formed, not friendships, they were too far gone into their pain for that. Allegiances is probably the best word. The souls are not the only inhabitants of the amulet. It may be that the madness they experience takes form, or perhaps there were already entities there. Inside the world of the amulet are creatures that harry the spirit, over time there is less and less of the druid attached to the soul." He rubbed his arms. It looked to me like it was to ensure they were real.

Dionne took his hand and said, "Lionel, you are home now."

He patted her hand. "Yes, I believe it. But it is like a wish so long hoped for that you don't trust the reality. Now, I'm wasting time. I met the druids, but they could not explain why they were trapped in the amulet. They claim they were not murdered, that they are not dead. I did not attempt to convince them that it was true. It seemed cruel."

"They are not," Trahaearn announced.

That got our attention. "What? We were told that the souls were there to protect them because they'd been murdered. Like the vampires were murdered by humans."

"Before I left, I was able to find one spirit who could still provide coherent information."

Lionel held up his hand. "Before you continue, you need to know that there is a spirit in there who is not a druid. Does that mean they are all still alive?" Hope echoed through his words.

Trahaearn answered, "Yes, we saw that. I do not know for certain if the sprite's body is alive. Perhaps the spirit is held past physical death, but—"

"We need to know, because one of the six is trapped there. If his body is dead, we will not be able to make the prophecy happen, and that means Dionne will not survive."

I looked at her. She seemed to take the news too well. "Dionne, we will make the prophecy happen."

She grinned. "I have no doubt. But if it is not to be, then it is not to be. Who was it that said prophecy cannot be controlled? You. One of the things I've learned from being a foster child is to deal with what is, and don't try to control anything."

"I told you she was a perceptive woman," Trahaearn said. "We will all do everything in our power to keep you alive, Dionne. Perhaps when we are finished with my task, we will know the fate of your trapped colleague."

None of this made me feel confident. I was grateful not to have to deal with Dionne in a panic, but I couldn't quell my own rising fears. "I suppose we need to figure out how to help you."

Trahaearn clapped his hands together and stood. "It appears so. That you have forgotten that I also learned something while I was in the amulet. I know why I have not been able to find the grove in Vancouver. It is because the bodies that belong to the druid souls in the amulet have been possessed by vampires."

10

"What?" I couldn't believe what he'd just said. "How can you be so sure that the spirit was sane enough to be telling you the truth? Perhaps it was a fantasy of the madness?"

Trahaearn glared at me, but instead of answering me, he said, "It does explain everything. I feel the pain that the souls feel, but cannot find the druids because there are none. A druid is both his spirit and his body. I have no doubt that it's the truth."

"That makes our agreement different." It felt like we were rushing into a disaster that we couldn't avoid or stop. "I have no love for the local drui— vampires, I guess. But how will they survive? Will we just loose the vampire souls to the atmosphere? Can we—"

Trahaearn slammed his hand on the counter. "We will free my people from that prison."

Lionel dug around in his bowl, clearly not wanting to get involved in the discussion. Dionne placed her hands on ours and waited until we were both looking at her. "I don't think that Quinn was trying to get out of the deal." She let our hands free and moved the tea mugs away from the danger zone. "Trahaearn, you know this is a game changer. It needs to be talked through."

He had calmed down a bit. I could only imagine how hard this was for him to hear, and I was going to make some sort of peace offering. Before I could, he drew in a deep breath and let it go before saying, "I agree. I am not immune to the effect of this news. The pain I felt is now stronger. The souls call me to hurry their release. I know that this is not what we agreed to, but I know that it needs to be done. If you wish to be freed from the obligation, I will release you with no repercussions. I can do this myself."

Someone save me from agreeable druids. I got the message. If I wanted out, he would let me go. What worried me was that he would withhold the information he had on the prophecy. "Our agreement was more complicated than that. And your news is not the only information we've received. I don't wish to be released from the obligation, but we need to discuss it."

There was a clunk from beside me and I turned to see Lionel passed out on the counter. I gave him a gentle shake and helped him to rise. "This discussion needs to wait until we have Lionel tucked in."

Trahaearn ran his hands through his hair, as though he was rubbing away pain. "Very well, but I will not wait until he is rested. These tasks we have set ourselves are urgent. We must make plans now."

I didn't answer until I'd helped Lionel climb into bed. When I returned to the kitchen, Dionne and Trahaearn were waiting expectantly. "We can come to an agreement without Lionel. I would prefer that the solution only involved you and me, Trahaearn."

Before I could add more, Dionne blurted out, "Hey, I should have some say in this."

I held up a hand and glared at her. "Let me finish. I would

prefer it, but I know that Dionne will not step back, and Lionel will want to be there to help."

Trahaearn looked at Dionne and said, "Something tells me that if we do not include both of your apprentices, we will fail." He clapped his hands together and rubbed them vigorously. "Let us get this planned. We should free my druids tonight. I worry that the vampires are aware that we have been into the amulet."

Freeing the druid souls meant putting them back in their bodies. A body would not survive having two souls that were sane, let alone one that was crazed from centuries of living in a prison. I had no love of the vampires either for how they had behaved with us, or their act of stealing the bodies. But they were the only ones of their kind left. What would happen to magic if they were destroyed completely? "Is there a way to save the vampires?"

"Wait." Dionne stood and paced the living room. We watched her, I had no idea what Trahaearn was thinking, but this was a new face of my apprentice. She was working through what she needed to say rather than just blurting out the first thing on her mind.

"Okay," she said as she rushed back to us. "There's something we aren't dealing with and we need to. What happens if the sprite disappears when you free the druids? What if something goes wrong? The prophecy is in danger here. I know you think that I'm worried because it's my life. That's not it. There's this feeling in here." She drove her fist into her stomach seeming oblivious to the pain she must have caused. "It must happen. We can't wait another fifty years, or whatever it is."

I led her to the chair and made her sit. "Don't be so sure what we are thinking. As one of the six, you are precious to us all. Not just me and Lionel, you are precious to all of the Real Folk." I hoped Trahaearn would not argue that point.

He handed her a glass of water. "You bring up an important point, Dionne. We have a problem. If the vampires are in contact with those inside the amulet, they will know we have freed Lionel and may take action to stop us. It is clear to me that they are trying to stop the prophecy by holding one of the six prisoner. I do not think we should delay simply to find a way to save them."

I patted Dionne's shoulder. "I think we need to act on the prophecy first, but how will we free the sprite. If his body is gone, we need him to inhabit someone so he can take part." I would deal with his attitude about the vampires later.

Trahaearn glanced at Lionel's closed door.

"No," I said, louder than I intended. "I will not agree to send him back."

"Quinn, it should be his decision," Dionne said. "You know he will want to do the right thing."

I knew he wouldn't hesitate. That didn't stop me wishing there was another way. "We need him to rest first. He must survive this. I think that means we need to be quick, but not be foolish." And I needed to stop worrying that the prophecy would trap him in the amulet forever.

Trahaearn held out his hand. I could see the tattoos pulse. "Our new agreement. I will help you with the prophecy and you will assist me in repairing the damage that has been done to my grove. And with the impostors."

I hesitated. His words left too much open, I need to make sure that the first option with the vampires wasn't death. I held out my hand. "The prophecy will be completed, and then we will find a solution to your problem with the vampires. We will not rush to murder them in revenge. We will only kill if there is no other option. I will not waste Real Folk lives."

He looked at me and I couldn't tell what he was thinking. "The vampires were not so squeamish."

Frustrated, I counted to ten before answering. "I am not them. It is not justice to kill for the past acts. Justice is about what we will do, not what they have done."

He paused, and I could see him trying to weigh what I had

said against what he wanted. He reached forward to take my hand.

"Hold on," Dionne said. "Don't I get to shake on this? I mean I'm one of the six after all."

I rolled my eyes at Trahaearn's expression. If there were any more interruptions, I swear he'd start punching holes in the wall. "See what I have to put up with?"

He laughed, the exasperation evaporating with the sound.

I gave her a stern look. This time she wouldn't wiggle out of the rules we set. "Dionne, as my apprentice you are bound by any agreement I make that doesn't explicitly exclude you. As one of the six, you have no choice in the prophecy. Until it is complete, you are its tool."

Irritation flashed across her face. "Crap. I thought I had to wait until I was eighteen to get some control over my life. Now it seems like I'll die an old woman before I get to make my own decisions. Fine, go ahead and make your agreement."

Understanding of her need to grow up didn't mean I could let her out of the apprentice oath. "I've done what I can think of to protect you. It is the best thing to do. When the prophecy is complete, even though you will still be my apprentice, and under-age, I promise you will have a bigger say in your life."

"Fine," she said. Her tone casual, but I could see the smile creep onto her lips. I hoped I wouldn't come to regret my promise.

"We have an agreement, then," Trahaearn said and we clasped hands and slapped shoulders to seal the bargain.

When we pulled apart, the weight of the future dropped on my shoulders. "We need to get this done today, but I think we need to rest first. Dionne, prepare the tea I taught you. Make it strong enough to give us two hours' sleep."

11

The rest had worked, at least for me. I was ready to face
the horror of the amulet again. What I didn't feel ready
to face was telling Lionel he had to go back. I scrubbed
the sleep from my eyes and joined the conversation already going
on the living room.

Dionne was talking to Trahaearn, and to my surprise, Lionel
had joined them.

"Hey, Quinn," Dionne said. "Are you ready? Lionel says he'd
rather get it over with, if he has to go back."

I looked at Lionel. He seemed calm, too calm. Perhaps his
mind was damaged during his stay in the amulet, leaving him
unable to feel fear. He grinned at me. "Don't look so worried. It
will only be for a short time, and I know you can come and get me
when it's done. It will make a difference."

It was a relief not to be the one who had to tell him and it felt
cowardly to be relieved. He sounded confident, but I wasn't
convinced. "What if it takes days to get the other four of the six
to come together? What if—"

"Don't plant that in your apprentice." Trahaearn looked at me
as if I were the mad one.

Dionne frowned at me and Lionel rolled his eyes. "Fine," I said, shrugging. "Everything will go as planned, and we'll be drinking beer at Banks before the day is out."

"Perhaps not that fast," Trahaearn said. "We need to prepare Lionel for the exchange, and we need to decide what to do with the sprite while he has possession of the body. We don't want him running off to the park and acting like a sprite."

"Yes, I would appreciate having my body in one piece when I get it back," Lionel said. "Have you decided what to do with the sprite when the prophecy is done? I would hate to let it die if we don't have a plan. And I would hate to send it back to the amulet."

Trahaearn didn't meet Lionel's eyes. We hadn't come up with a plan for the future of the sprite. I was ashamed that I hadn't even thought about it. Surely the sprite deserved as much of my caring as the vampires. "We'll have to find a way to give the sprite a home. Beacon will help."

Lionel brightened. "Have you asked Beacon? Does Moss know what is going on?"

"Not yet," I said. "We can ask before we send you back." It would give me a few hours at least to find a way to guarantee our success.

"No. We can ask when the sprite is here," Trahaearn answered. "It will be better if we get the sprite out with no delay."

As much as I wanted to, I couldn't marshal an argument against it.

Lionel stretched, and I heard his joints crack under the strain. "Man, it's nice to feel your body react to moving. In there... well it's like you have an itch, but there's nothing to scratch."

"Are you sure you'll be okay?" I still couldn't reconcile myself to sending him back. "It might be as long this time as it was before."

He scowled. "Quinn, we don't have a choice. Either I go back or the prophecy won't happen and Dionne will die. And I don't know how I would live through that, if I did nothing to prevent it."

He was right. The events of the last day had gotten me on edge. Between The Morrigan's veiled announcement that the truth was coming, and Trahaearn's arrival, too many things felt like they were coming to an end. Having Lionel back was more like a beginning. I closed my eyes and focused on the bright side. In the next couple of days, all the pressures we had been living under would be gone. We'd have time to teach Dionne about all of our ways, and grow her skills. She wouldn't be in such a rush to learn that she would lie to everyone and bring Ms. Metcalfe to our door. And maybe, with the druid souls returned, we would have access to a library of information that was currently closed. "Okay. What's the plan?"

Trahaearn beckoned me to sit. "We had not made a plan. You were only a few minutes behind us in waking. Perhaps I can share my thoughts, and we can start there."

Relieved that everyone seemed to be reasonable, I said, "Okay, let's hear your ideas."

"We have already been in there so the shock will be less, but don't think it will be easy this time. I think if we return to the exact positions that we used to bring Lionel back, we should be able to pass his soul to the amulet when we find the sprite."

"So, I don't have to cast the two spells again?" Dionne asked. "Hey, how did the slowing spell end? It just went away when your spirit came back, right?"

Lionel looked at his hands. "I think the spell that froze my body in time only worked because my spirit was gone. I don't think it works on live bodies. I'm glad you don't have to use the other spell to send me into the amulet."

"Why?" Dionne asked concerned. "Did it hurt? I didn't think about it hurting you."

He shuddered. "Not exactly, but I was unprepared. And you do not want to enter a place like the amulet unprepared." His gaze seemed to take in her real worry that she'd done something to harm him. "Dionne, you did what you had to do. I survived, right?"

She didn't answer, just kept her eyes on him as though searching for reassurance that he wasn't broken.

"What do you mean, a place like the amulet?" I asked.

"As bad as it was, I chose to explore while I still had some sanity. At the outer reaches of the world, there were echoes of other souls. Not our kind of beings, but perhaps that's where the souls come from. Perhaps where Ranseed inhabits. I don't know."

Trahaearn patted his knee. "You are right. The amulet is one of many such dimensions. I don't know if it is worse, or better, or if it is simply the same as the others. But there will be no one in there when we are done. The amulet will be destroyed, if possible. I swear to you that is one world that no one will ever endure again."

Lionel seemed to drift away for a moment. Then he shook himself and came back to us. "That may not be possible. But we can make those plans later. If we enter the amulet in the way you describe, how will the exchange of souls happen? Will I need to do anything?"

Trahaearn shrugged. "This is not something I have experienced before. I know it is possible to switch souls in that world, but I have never done this with only one body."

"Then I need to tell you that you may force me from this body if needed. I cannot guarantee that I will be able to volunteer to leave when we get there."

Dionne sobbed a breath. "Lionel, maybe we can find another way. I don't want you to—"

He hugged her. "Dionne, I am willing to do this. I just can't guarantee my conviction will survive the journey. Don't back out on this. I'll be very angry with you if I wake up in this body when the spell is over." He wiped a tear from her cheek.

"Fine. I'll just owe you a giant favor when it's over." She pulled her hair back and knotted it. "Unless anyone has a better idea, let's get this done. I have to go home at some point tonight."

I had nothing to add. It was hard to create the kind of plan I wanted, one that had some potential for success, when we had no path to follow, no experience to fall back on. "Everyone get ready. Dionne, Lionel, put on some warmer clothes. We may be down there for a few hours. I don't want you catching a cold."

While they were digging through Lionel's coats for something comfortable, I told Trahaearn, "If it comes to a choice, and you can sacrifice me, then do it. I only ask that you ensure Lionel becomes a wizard and Dionne completes the prophecy."

He slapped me on the back. "Are you always so determined that things will go wrong?"

I tried to laugh, but couldn't quite lift the feeling of gloom. "If you had lived through the last year of my life, you might feel differently about the odds of something going wrong."

We settled onto the bare earth of my workroom. Lionel offered to cast the circle, perhaps he missed magic. I could sympathize. When I couldn't see, I'd missed magic more than my sight until I figured out how to do small spells that couldn't do much damage if I got them wrong.

In the short time we'd been absent, more of the sunken power had resurfaced. "It won't be quite as uncomfortable this time," I said as we all placed some bare portion of skin on the dirt.

"Physically, yes. Let's carry that comfort in our minds as we enter the amulet." Trahaearn took my hand and waited until I had Dionne's in mine. Lionel turned his head to let his cheek lie on the ground.

The circle complete, Trahaearn started the chant that bonded our hands. This time he didn't pause, and we were inside the amulet before I could brace myself.

The light was brilliant and painful. There was no place that we could look to avoid the searing blaze of white. The screams of the souls filled my head like a violent case of tinnitus. I knew my body wasn't with me, but it felt like my ears were bleeding, and my eyes, but that might have been tears. We'd landed right in the middle of the amulet this time. No chance to get used to the chaos as we approached.

I struggled to think of a way to clear a path in the madness. If we couldn't find a measure of calm, we might not be able to find the sprite and return to our world. There was no way I could live with leaving Lionel here.

"It will pass," Lionel's voice slid through the screams. "It is like this for a short time, and then the normal madness returns."

As his words faded, the light dimmed and the screams diminished. Eventually, the sounds became bearable, and I understood the meaning of normal madness. As my sight returned, I saw Lionel standing in front of Trahaearn, not holding anyone's hand, but still tethered to Dionne and Trahaearn with wisps of mist.

"Well, now we're here, what do we do to bring the sprite to us?" Dionne asked the question that was forming in my mind. "And can we do it before we have to go through that again?"

Trahaearn looked to Lionel. "Can you sense him?"

I watched Lionel's Adam's apple bob as he swallowed. I could feel the fear radiate from him even as he tried to gain control of it. His courage awed me with its silence. "I can feel him at the edge. Can I go to him? Will I be able to find you again?"

Trahaearn looked into the distance. "Only you can know that, but Dionne found us last time."

I glanced at Dionne. "You aren't going to leave again."

"No, Quinn. I'll stay." Her voice quavered with fear. I tried not to hear an echo of the unspoken words... unless I have to go.

Trahaearn leaned forward. "Lionel, can you try to call the sprite first? Don't say why you need him. We don't know what the other souls will do if they know what is going to happen. I don't have any control over them in here."

Lionel nodded, then his lips moved as though he were calling someone. I couldn't hear him, but I hoped the sprite would hear and respond.

As we waited, other souls flew at us. Some circled Dionne, but most seemed attracted to Trahaearn. I tried to hold back the shivers I felt every time a shred of vapor passed through me. I wasn't as successful as I hoped. My apprentices were putting me to shame with their courage.

"I think you'll need to go find him," Trahaearn finally said. "I cannot get any sense from these others. We will wait until you return."

Lionel looked around and suddenly disappeared. I could still feel Dionne and Trahaearn's hand in mine so I trusted that they held his body. Knowing I was only here in spirit didn't stop me from holding my breath. I started counting. The only thing I could think of to keep me sane.

More wraiths circled then vanished. I could see Trahaearn muttering as each approached, but nothing changed in the way they flashed between visibility and invisibility. Some formed faces, the only expression showing was pain.

My count reached a hundred with no sign of Lionel. "Is there something you can do, Trahaearn? Should I go looking for him?"

Trahaearn's hand tightened on mine. "Quinn, stay with us. Remember the last time. I do not wish to be standing here waiting for you to return. You do not know the sprite. You will only become another reason for us to stay. Or another soul abandoned here until we can free everyone."

I watched Dionne as she muttered under her breath. I could see that she burned to run for Lionel in the way her body seemed to twitch with pent up energy.

By the time I'd counted to two hundred, I was starting to think I was drowning in the madness surrounding us.

At three hundred, I stopped worrying about breathing and started worrying that we would be here forever.

As I reached four hundred, I wondered if we'd been here so

long that Ms. Metcalfe had broken into my house and was standing over our bodies in my basement.

I was starting to find the whole situation funny as I counted five hundred. Then I wondered if that was the first step into madness.

I made it to six hundred and wondered how Lionel had managed to stay sane here.

Then he was back.

"I found the sprite. He didn't believe me at first. I had to explain everything. I'm sorry it took so long." Even without his body, he sounded out of breath.

We waited for Lionel to continue but he didn't. "Is it coming?"

"Oh, yes. It will be here soon. I'm not sure why it wouldn't follow me back. It said something about not wanting to draw evil to us." He glanced around again. "So, what happens when he gets here?"

Trahaearn turned away from the wisp of vapor that was screaming silence. "You will have to make the transfer. We will leave, you stay, and the sprite will follow us."

"Are you sure it will be that easy?" I wanted it to be true. I was so used to being the one in control, that I didn't trust it when I wasn't.

"It should be. The sprite should be eager to leave. Lionel is committed to the exchange. There are no barriers that I can see." Trahaearn looked worried despite his words.

"So, we just wait again?" Dionne's voice was strained.

Trahaearn grinned at her. "Yes, it's a good lesson in patience. I wish it was not such a frightful place."

I shared my suggestion about counting. Perhaps it would help them more than it had me. I couldn't help starting my own count again; at least it passed time.

Either I was getting used to the amulet, a thought I didn't care for, or the sprite came fast. As it approached, I heard a change in the background sounds. The screams didn't stop, they hushed. The sprite's soul was bright yellow, and was gaining mass as it approached. It was like the years were reversing, and the shreds of its being were being drawn back together.

It overshot us, and then swung back.

"Go, go, go, go, go." The words were high pitched. "It comes."

Trahaearn muttered something and then asked, "What comes?"

"It. The thing. We go."

"Wait," Dionne said. "Will Lionel be safe?" The sprite draped itself over her head. "Get out. It's not me."

It lifted from her and hovered in front of us.

"There's some kind of danger on its way," she said. "It's not clear how long we have, but since the other souls seem to be leaving, maybe we should too."

She looked around, and I could see there was fear, then suddenly nothing. "That was weird. It was like I knew everything the sprite did, then it was gone."

"Lionel, do you know anything about this danger?" I wouldn't leave him here without knowing he would be safe.

"It's a bogeyman," he said. "I heard about it now and then, but nothing came of it."

I wasn't sure I believed him, but I wasn't going to argue in this environment. "Stay safe while you are here."

He glanced over his shoulder. "Yes, Quinn. I'll find an empty place. There are plenty."

Trahaearn pulled our focus back to him. "If you are ready, we will start the transfer."

I nodded and waited for instruction.

He looked around as though hearing something approach. I couldn't see anything through the madness around us. "Dionne, you seem to have some control over the sprite. Can you keep him calm while we proceed?"

The sprite was hovering and spinning in front of us, emitting a shrill whistle. It was slightly better than the shrieks we'd been listening to, but I was looking forward to being able to tell it to shut up.

"I'll try," she said. "No guarantees."

His glance flicked to the cloud that was the sprite. "Lionel, I need you to relax your hold on your body. I will remove my hand from your body and reach toward the sprite. At that time, you should exchange your souls."

I didn't like the sound of that. "Should? I thought you knew what you were doing."

Trahaearn dismissed me with a shake of his head. "It hasn't been done before. There is no reason it will fail. Let's get it over with."

It was my fault. I'd taken a backseat to him on this whole endeavor. I'm not sure why I gave him so much credit, but that would change as soon as we got home. I wasn't going to sit back and watch as he took over my apprentices.

In here, our souls were translucent, but shaped much like we were outside the amulet, probably because we had bodies. Outside, we were sitting close and touching. In here, we moved independently. Trahaearn raised his right hand and touched the sprite. The world faded and then we were back in my workroom.

"Don't change position until we know who is in Lionel's body." Trahaearn's words stopped me from letting go of my contact with him and Dionne.

I glanced at what I could see of Lionel's face, it was paper white and dull. I'd seen that look before — on dead bodies. "Something went wrong. We have to go back."

Dionne squeezed my fingers. "Is anyone there, Trahaearn?"

I watched as the druid closed his eyes and muttered a few words. He shook his head. "Quinn is right. Neither the sprite nor Lionel has returned. We need to go back to the amulet and try again."

"How will we know this time will be successful? We can't keep Dionne all night, and we can't let her leave if no one inhabits the body." Why did I feel like something was trying to trap us in that world?

Dionne glared at me. "I'm not leaving until this is fixed. I won't abandon Lionel, or the sprite."

The force of her magic glowed through her words giving it the power of oath.

"Stop," Trahaearn hissed. "We will return with a soul this time. If needed, we will bring Lionel back so that Dionne can disengage. Then we will return for the sprite. Quinn, do not bring negative thoughts to this circle."

"Let's just go now." I knew it wasn't going to get any better until we had a spirit in this body. "We'll get it right so there'll be no problem. Dionne, we have a few hours left before you must leave." I turned my attention to Trahaearn. "If we don't send her home, we may get a visit from social services. That means we won't be able to bring on the prophecy, or deal with the vampires. So, consider what I say to be incentive to get it right, not negative thoughts."

Trahaearn's look chilled me. The arrogance might be okay in his druid grove, but this was my home and so far, he'd been less than perfect with his attempts to sort out the problems. I would deal with his attitude later.

"Close your eyes and picture us in the amulet." He waited until we'd both followed his instructions.

We were back in the madness in the space of a breath. This time I noticed the wind. It swirled around us coming from one side bearing ice, and the other scorching my skin. We were alone.

"I'll find Lionel," Dionne said then vanished.

"What will you do when she has fulfilled the prophecy? Then she will no longer be an apprentice." Trahaearn's tone was neutral, but I couldn't help feel some kind of judgment in his words.

I gritted my teeth at the truth of his question. "She doesn't know that. I thought I would try to get her to agree to remain a student. She wants to leave the human world. Perhaps that will be worth it to her."

He laughed. "I wish you luck."

We waited, and waited. Then at the edge of my sight I saw a whirl of smoke. Dionne reappeared. "He's coming and so is Inlackt."

"Who is Inlackt?" I heard Trahaearn's echo of my question.

"The sprite," she said as if we should have known. "Lionel has been talking to him. He's agreed to come with us."

Lionel's spirit arrived as she finished speaking. "I've explained everything. He's ready to go." The vapor forming his soul was stretched out and beginning to tatter on the edges.

Trahaearn held out his hand. "Lionel, we will be as fast as possible, but it will likely be a couple of days."

"I will be fine. Or as fine as I can be here. Hurry before something goes wrong. I'll be listening for your call when you come back." The cloud of vapor whirled away from us.

"Hurry, Trahaearn," Dionne urged. "There is something here that wants to stop us."

A ball of golden smoke curled around Trahaearn's hand. "No, Inlackt, it is not my body we have for you. Stay with us and we will have a home for you in a moment."

This time the transition back to my workroom was slower. Disoriented, as though I were falling from a height, I slipped back in my body. Lionel stirred in front of me, and Dionne let go of my hand to place both of hers on Lionel's body.

"It's done," Trahaearn announced.

"Help... Help... Help... Where... me..." the words stuttered out of Lionel's mouth, but the voice was higher than usual. It piped more than spoke, and the sound turned into a keening as it progressed.

12

Dionne reached for Lionel's head. It was impossible for me to think of this as anyone other than Lionel. I had to keep telling myself, that the terror we heard wasn't his. It was a sprite's terror. There was no telling how long he had been in the amulet, or how insane he was. We had to hope that the prophecy didn't need the six to be sane. Or, at least not all of them.

"You are safe," she murmured as if to a frightened child. "We won't let anything happen to you."

Trahaearn stood and broke the circle. "Let's get him off the cold floor. Maybe some warmth will help."

I helped him lift the body. Dionne continued to make soothing noises as we placed him on the couch. "I don't want him to hurt Lionel's body. I'll try a sleep spell." She said it as if asking permission.

I was gratified that she looked to me for that permission, not Trahaearn. Then I felt petty for enjoying what only I saw as a victory. "It should work on the spirit rather than the body. I've never really thought of it in those terms before."

"No, we don't usually think of a body and a soul being two

80

different entities," Trahaearn said. "Let's give Dionne a little time to try healing him first. She has strength in that."

I reluctantly sat back and watched as Dionne perched on the edge of the couch. She was speaking so quietly that all I could hear was a gentle murmur of sound. Her hand stroked Lionel's forehead and the pleading softened to a mewl.

She looked at us. "He is calmer. I need to tell him what is happening. I think giving him the truth might be the best thing."

Trahaearn nodded at the same time I did. "Before you do that, let us get into position to restrain him."

Dionne's eyes darkened. "Don't hurt him. No matter what happens, this is Lionel's body. I want to return it in the same condition he left it in."

I patted her shoulder. "We won't. This is just a precaution. I don't want him lashing out and hurting you. Even if you have him soothed, he isn't used to using a body this size."

She nodded and moved to the side, keeping her fingertips in contact with Lionel's forehead.

Trahaearn held Lionel's feet down. His hands barely touching the exposed skin, but the muscles in his arms tensed, ready for action. I placed my hands on Lionel's shoulders and braced myself. "Go ahead."

Dionne bent to speak in Lionel's ear. "Inlackt, do you know where you are?"

His body twitched under my fingers. I resisted the urge to tighten my grip.

"In a body. One that is too big."

Dionne retreated a little and spoke again. "Yes, you are borrowing my friend's body. We need you to help bring the prophecy to fruition."

"This body only knows one magickkkk. Only one."

Dionne looked at Trahaearn. "Is that going to be a problem?"

He shook his head. "Not if he is the only one who is impaired. We must hope that the others are fully empowered."

She turned back to Inlackt. "Did you hear that?"

"Yessss." He squeezed Lionel's eyes shut. "Wait."

The twitching started again. This time I put more pressure on the shoulders.

"This body is mine?" The voice was less frantic, but the childish, wheedling tone was disconcerting in a body as large as Lionel's.

Dionne paled then took a deep breath. "No, you are borrowing it. You must return it to Lionel when we are done."

The twitching became violent. I slid my hands down Lionel's arms and held them still. Inlackt bucked under my grasp. I looked at Trahaearn, he was leaning his weight on Lionel's legs, pressing them into the cushions of the couch.

"No. I have this body. I am Lionel now. I will not go back. I am free. I I I I." Joy shone in the voice.

I muttered a spell and the words cut off. Dionne looked at me, accusation shining from her eyes. "I could have helped him."

I motioned for Trahaearn to let go of his grip. "He'll sleep. It's probably best that his mind rests. Dionne, I know you could have done something, but we don't have the time you need."

"How can we make the prophecy happen if he's crazy?" Tears strained her words.

I took the blanket we'd used to hide Lionel before, and draped it over Inlackt. "Think about what it's like for him. We see Lionel, and that seems like a safe haven to us. All Inlackt sees is the change of one prison for another. Lionel's body is as foreign to him as the amulet. He needs time to realize it's not a place of madness. And time to figure out how to work the body."

She wiped her eyes. "I know what he's feeling. I was there with him."

Trahaearn took her arm. "Let's go upstairs. I think Inlackt is not the only one who needs a rest. The amulet has its effect on us, too. And I am sure the thought that Lionel is still trapped there weighs upon us."

13

I settled Dionne on a stool. It was already late afternoon, and we had a lot of work ahead of us.

Tea was the strongest thing I would allow Dionne to take while she was living with humans. I placed the honey jar on the counter. "Sweeten it as much as you can stand. The sugar will help to dispel the melancholy you feel from that place."

Dionne stirred two spoonfuls into the dark tea. "I know I can heal him, Quinn. Trahaearn said I was strong in healing. I know it will be better for the prophecy that way."

Trahaearn sat beside her. "Dionne, I think you are right that Inlackt needs to be sane. But I think he's missing direction, and it's not about healing. It would be better if one of his own were able to connect with him."

"Moss, would be the best, but we would have to take Inlackt to him. He's too big now to leave the park." I tried to imagine us getting away with taking the sprite to the park and couldn't.

"I could get Beacon," Dionne said. "If he's going to be taking over from Moss, he probably has some sway over the sprites. Even if Inlackt was in the amulet for so long that he doesn't know Beacon, it might work."

Trahaearn asked who Moss and Beacon were. When I answered, he said, "Despite his knowledge of Moss, I am not sure that the sprite is even from this area. But it is a good idea. How long do you think it would take?"

I held up my hand. "Wait. We can't just send her to Stanley Park to dig around the trees for Beacon. It's too dangerous. If she's seen, it could attract the wrong attention."

Dionne sighed. "Ms. Metcalfe isn't likely to be hanging around the park. And even if she is, I'm supposed to be here today."

Impatience battled with caution for control. "Ms. Metcalfe isn't the only person we need to worry about. What if the vampires know we've removed Inlackt? What if they see you and... I don't know kidnap you?"

Her confidence shattered as she thought about what they might do to her. "They would kill me," she said quietly. "And you wouldn't know. And Lionel would stay in the amulet."

I felt like a jerk for reminding her of the real dangers, but she needed a clear head. Optimism and confidence could get her into real trouble right now.

"Maybe you should go," she said.

Satisfied that she wouldn't take too many risks, I relented. "No. You can do this, but you need to be careful. We'll put a glamor on you first."

"Fine," Dionne said, jumping off her stool, dread immediately replaced with enthusiasm. "I can do that. Maybe Bud will be around to help me find Beacon."

I stood her in the middle of the living room. It was long past time to trust her magic. "Cast your own glamor. Make yourself old and bent."

Trahaearn and I watched as she focused the spell and, before our eyes, withered into a hag.

She finished and turned to us, hunched and moving stiffly. "Is this okay?"

I laughed. "You look great but remember to disguise your voice."

She swallowed, cleared her throat, and then said in a creaky voice, "Yes, youngster. Now, I think I just need to get to the park and find an imp, or a fairy, to help."

Trahaearn handed her a slip of paper. "If you can't find him quickly, use this spell. But only use it if you need to. I understand that sprites of power don't like to be summoned."

She scanned the paper and then stuffed it into her pocket. "I'll be back as fast as I can. I don't think Beacon or Moss will want to leave a sprite in this state."

She ran to the door, slowing to a hobble before I could remind her of her disguise.

Trahaearn returned to the kitchen. "Have you any more beer?"

"Sorry, no. I can't exactly send Dionne to buy some." I put the kettle on to make a fresh pot of tea, then turned off the gas. "No, we have time to get some beer and groceries if we're fast." I grabbed my wallet and we walked the few blocks to the store.

WE BEAT DIONNE BACK TO THE HOUSE BY TEN MINUTES, JUST enough time to put the beer in the fridge and the groceries in the cupboard. Beacon followed her through the door, bending to avoid rubbing his head against the ceiling. He'd grown a foot since I last saw him. His size was a good indicator of how close he was to becoming the leader of the sprites. Our days of visiting with Beacon outside the park were numbered. I would miss him. Moss would be shrinking at the same pace. He'd melt into the earth on the day that Beacon took over.

"Let's get this done," Beacon said before we could introduce him to Trahaearn. "Dionne filled me in. There'll be time for small talk when we're finished. And time for one of those beers, when they're cold."

This was a new Beacon. The old one was more laid back,

always willing to help, but never ready to take control. Now he was going to be king of the sprites, he needed to be stronger, but it was going to take some getting used to.

Dionne rushed to open the door to the basement. "Have you checked on him?"

Lionel's body was in the same position we'd left him. Dionne placed her hand on his forehead and nodded. "He's sleeping. Maybe that will be all he needs." She looked up to me. "Do you think he got any sleep in there, the amulet?"

"Maybe," I said. "Let Beacon get to him and we'll see."

She pulled away from the body, and Beacon settled on the floor in front of the couch. He placed his hands on Lionel's head and closed his eyes. After a few minutes, he opened them and shook his head. "All I get is gibberish."

Dionne joined him on the floor. "Does he know who you are?"

He looked at her with that 'think it through' expression and waited.

"Oh, yeah, maybe if I introduce you." She giggled and then took control of herself. Placing her fingertips on Lionel's arm she whispered, "Inlackt, can you hear me?"

We all waited for the reply. When a few minutes had passed with no response, I said, "Dionne, maybe we need to try something else."

She looked away from Lionel and said, "Oh, he's there, I'm trying to get him to agree to talk to Beacon."

Beacon leaned forward and placed his hands on hers. He frowned in concentration and then removed his hands and nodded. "I need you as a conduit, Dionne. Will you be okay if I talk through you?"

She settled into a more comfortable position. "Do what you need to do. The last time I talked to him, he was pretty far gone. There isn't much improvement now."

Beacon turned to us. "Quinn, I think you need to be in the

link, but I don't know you Trahaearn. I would prefer you stay outside this spell."

A flash of annoyance crossed the druid's face, but it was quickly replaced by a smile. "Why don't I go out into the garden and replenish myself while you do what is needed." He turned to leave without another word.

Beacon watched him go and listened to the floor creak as Trahaearn crossed the kitchen. "Are you sure about him?"

Good question. Was I? "He's proven what he can do. He brought Lionel back, and knows things about the prophecy, and promised to help us."

Beacon turned his attention to Lionel's body. "I hope he does help, but he did send Lionel back. Are you okay with that?"

"That was because of me," Dionne said. "Lionel will be back when the prophecy is complete. I guess we need to know what can be done for Inlackt when that happens." She held out her hand. "Let me introduce you to him."

Beacon reached for her hand and then took mine, completing the link. "His name is Inlackt?"

I answered while Dionne made the connection. "That's what he said."

"Inlackt was a friend of Moss. He disappeared over a hundred years ago. If he knows that, it might be impossible for him to gain sanity. He'll know his body is gone and there's no way back."

"He knows," Dionne whispered in our minds. "You can talk to him directly. If you need anything from us, just ask."

I closed my eyes and entered the link. It was dark. Three lights glowed, one warm green, one a welcoming yellow, and one a pulsing red. "Inlackt," Beacon called gently. "I am Beacon. Moss's grandson. Heir to the park. Will you come to speak with me?"

The red light seemed to flow toward us. "Moss, still lives?" The question ended on a cackle. "Dead, dead, dead."

"You still live," Beacon assured the sprite. "It may be a different kind of life, but it is still life."

"No. I do not want to live this way."

Inlackt's voice was steadier, but now it carried a taint of depression. I bit my tongue to stop myself saying he had to make the prophecy happen. Beacon must have sensed my fear because he glared at me. I wasn't used to him being so... commanding wasn't the right word, but it would do.

"Inlackt, you know that you are one of the six."

"Yesssss."

"The others have come into their powers. You need to represent the sprites for this."

"Yessss. But I am not me."

"Will you accept my guidance?"

"You are not Moss."

"No, but Moss is declining, and I am ascending. As is natural, Moss will return to the earth."

"Moss is my leader."

"Very well, sleep now."

We relaxed and disengaged from each other. I saw the strain on Beacon's face.

He winced as he straightened his body. "Growing pains," he said rubbing his knees. "We have a problem."

"No kidding," I said. "Do you have any way to apply your authority?"

"Quinn, we can't force it," Dionne said.

Beacon stretched and groaned. "No. I will not force this. He sounds more sane, but I think that's just on the surface. Let's try again. This time, I want Dionne to do the talking. You need to convince him that I am the new leader."

She glanced at the window. "Would you let Trahaearn help? I'm not sure I can convince a sprite who he should obey."

"No. I still need to know more about this druid before I trust him enough to convince one of my sprites. This is not just a normal sprite, and California druids are very different from ours."

I felt like I was keeping a secret by not telling Beacon the truth about our own druids. It wasn't that I didn't trust him, or that I didn't believe Trahaearn. I just didn't think it was my job to spread the word. And it was probably prudent to make sure that the vampires didn't know we were aware of their deception.

"What do you want Dionne to do?" I could, at least, make sure that she was well instructed.

Beacon looked at Lionel's body before answering. I could see familiar feelings cross his face in the little frown and the slight shake of his head. He couldn't quite reconcile what he saw with what he knew. "I think he has some affinity for you, Dionne. Maybe because he is one of the six, maybe your healing energy, or maybe because you were there when he was rescued... Or maybe some combination of those things. You need to connect to that affinity. We need him to accept me. We can try for sane later."

"I'm willing. He needs to be cared for though. You won't just leave him when we're done, right?" Beacon assured her that he would never abandon any of his sprites. Apparently convinced, she switched places with Beacon and we remade the connection.

The view I had of Inlackt was subtly different. Where Beacon saw him as a part of a community, as one of his own people, Dionne saw Inlackt as a person. One who was wounded. This time the disconcerting double vision of magic and reality was gone. I could also see our regular bodies superimposed over the lights that represented our magic.

"Inlackt," she murmured. "Do you know me?"

"Yessssssss. You are the one. You will unite us."

She glanced at me and shrugged. "Do you trust me?"

"Trust is hard."

"Will you trust me?"

There was a long pause. It was as though Inlackt had gone somewhere to think. When he spoke, it seemed he was returning.

"I will trust you," he said. "I will hear you."

She sighed. "I am telling you to trust that Beacon is your... I don't know. I guess he is going to be what Moss is."

"How do you know, know, know?"

"I have known him for only a few weeks, and he has grown two feet in that time. I think that means he is growing into his power."

"Yes. That is how it has worked."

Her light glowed brighter. "Will you listen to him? Will you let him lead you?"

Another long pause. Beacon seemed to be waiting to see if he had passed a test. I guess it was one. If he couldn't get Inlackt to follow, could he lead anyone?

"Yessss," Inlackt finally responded.

She looked at Beacon who was smiling, he mouthed, *sleep*.

"You need rest. We will return when we need you. Sleep now, Inlackt. You are safe here."

Lionel's eyes closed. We broke the connection. Pain stabbed through my back and joints from sitting in one position for too long.

"We need to bring Trahaearn into this," I said. I expected Beacon to argue, but he just nodded.

14

I looked out into the garden to see Trahaearn lying face down on the small patch of grass between my herb garden and the tree where Cate's body was buried. There was no one around, but I did worry that someone would see him and wonder what this weirdo was doing. Or why I had a dead body in my garden. Humans don't like oddness.

Putting aside my worries about what the neighbors would think, I called him in. When I returned to the kitchen, Dionne had three bottles of beer on the counter and was spooning tea leaves into the steeping bag.

Beacon popped the top off a bottle and handed it to me, then handed an unopened bottle to Trahaearn. The druid gestured and the top sprang into his hand.

I took a long drink from my beer, then glanced over at Dionne who was grinning at the two as they established their territories.

"So now that we have Inlackt ready to take orders, what do we do next?" she asked.

"The prophecy," I answered. "We need to enact the prophecy as soon as we can, so we can get Lionel back where he belongs."

She poured the water into the pot. "And what happens to Inlackt then?"

Beacon put his bottle on the counter. "We need to work that out. I can't order him to enact the prophecy and then die. I won't. We need to find a way to preserve him."

Trahaearn didn't join the conversation. I watched as he studied each of us. If he had a plan, he wasn't ready to share it, and I didn't like him taking a back seat. "Trahaearn, do you have any suggestions?"

"Inlackt is Beacon's problem. I think the prophecy will be fine if he agrees to do his part. Even with only Lionel's magic, he is still one of the six. You can see it shining in him. Dionne is strong enough to make up the difference anyway."

Dionne joined us, steaming mug in hand. "Are you sure his power won't be needed? Why would it matter if one of us can have no access to their magic?"

He looked at his arm, the tattoos that now seemed alive, crawled along the skin. "When you reach my age, you know that there are no certainties in life. That includes prophecies. There are no guarantees that even with all six fully mature in their power, the prophecy would come to pass. It has not until now."

I hate it when people go into philosophical musings. "Dionne's life kind of hangs on the prophecy. If Inlackt were sane, we might have a better idea what he knows."

"I could heal him," Dionne said. "I know I can do it."

"No, you are not ready for such magic." I hadn't given her any training in healing. In truth, I hadn't given her much training at all.

"She is stronger than you believe, Quinn," Trahaearn said. "She may not be practiced, but she needs your trust more than she needs your lessons."

Dionne blushed at the praise. Resentment burned in my stomach. Who was he to tell me how to instruct my apprentice?

"I have taught many a young druid," he said. "I know how they hang balanced between ignorance and innocence. Dionne is smart enough to keep things in control, to know where she isn't capable, to take a risk."

"The risks are more than a normal apprentice faces." I felt like I was spinning between doing what was right and what was safe.

"You are both right," Beacon said. "She is unready, and she is capable. I know that, ideally, we would take our time. We would find a place for Inlackt to reside, we would have Lionel in his own body, we would take the time to train Dionne, and the druids would be more helpful." He stared at Trahaearn as he said the last.

It was a good time for Trahaearn to tell Beacon the truth, but he didn't.

"It seems to me we have nothing to lose," Dionne said. "Or I guess I mean, we risk losing everything no matter what we do, or don't do. I think it's better to risk doing something."

The confidence of the young. It made me remember that she was very young in terms of Real Folk. If she had been raised among us, she would have been in apprenticeship by the age of ten and be ready to graduate to full witch by the time she reached her twenties. In reality, she had no idea how her powers would develop, and little sense of her own mortality.

As reluctant as I was to admit it, she was right. We needed to do something. We needed to keep trying to succeed. We couldn't just wait for something to happen.

I looked at Beacon and wondered if he cared about Dionne, or if he was only concerned with the wellbeing of our mad sprite. And then I felt guilt. Beacon had never refused to help. No matter how much he had grown, or how close he was to taking over from Moss, he wouldn't have changed that much. I suppressed the voice in my head that was telling me to be careful. "Okay, you can try. How can we help?"

Dionne's eyes widened. "Are you serious?"

"Yes."

"Okay, well. I guess I need you all there with me. I might need to pull power from you, and I'll need you to make sure I don't get in too deep. I'm not sure I'll know when that happens. I don't want to end up like Inlackt. I won't be able to help Lionel come back if that happens."

Trahaearn lifted his bottle in a toast. "I'm in. I'll make sure you are safe, and you may take my power. I'll draw from the earth, so you don't have to worry about taking too much."

Beacon raised his own beer. "I don't think you can access my power, but if you need it to help Inlackt, you are welcome."

It was left to me. She was my apprentice and needed my guidance. "Let's get to it. I'll make sure you are safe. And I will give you what I can to guide you."

She shrugged, and then let a grin light her face. "Okay, let's get this done before I'm sent home."

We settled back in the workroom. Dionne arranged us around Lionel who was in the center of the circle. "I need to have access to power and to authority," she said placing Beacon and Trahaearn on either side of her.

My role was to monitor Dionne and Lionel's bodies. This was her first healing. We all worried that she wouldn't have the skill to balance the physical and the mental healing. Or maybe that was just me.

"Okay, everyone close your eyes and follow me in." The authority in her voice was at the same time heartening and disturbing. It made me optimistic that we would be successful as well as question how she learned to be that confident in her untested skills.

I sank into Inlackt's mind. We shared what could only have been his self-image. A scattering of light balls spinning in erratic circles around a shadowy form that wasn't quite sprite, but neither was it Lionel. It was disconcerting to watch, and worrisome to think that if he couldn't see himself as a cohesive whole, we were in trouble.

"Inlackt, we are here to help." Dionne formed an image of

herself as a glowing flame. Or perhaps that was also Inlackt's interpretation of her image.

One of the larger balls of light floated toward us. It hovered over Dionne then flashed through her, and my body jerked in response. Dionne's voice filled my head. "I am fine. You don't need to protect me right now."

I relaxed and watched as Dionne convinced Inlackt to draw his parts together, her voice disappeared as she worked. Following the action with only my sight was stressful. I would watch as Dionne's flame flickered, worrying that she was suffering, perhaps going mad as Inlackt's light grew. It took time, but I eventually noticed that the scattered light balls were fewer, and though his shape didn't settle on one body, it was getting brighter.

As Inlackt coalesced, I started to hear faint words, then I could hear Dionne clearly. "It is time," she murmured. "Come together and join us."

The largest ball of light started to spin. The action drawing the remaining sparks toward the center. When there was only one ball of light, I could hear his voice. "It feels good to be whole. I like this body, but where is the magic?"

"We will investigate that when we are together," Dionne said. "Are you ready?"

"Yes."

Dionne led us to the world, and it felt as though I was backing out of a room. Just as my own body surround me, I heard a giggle, and then the remaining light ball exploded.

"What was that?" I reached for Dionne. "Are you okay"

She blinked and then said, "I am, but we need to go back. He's not healed." She reached frantically for my hands. "Join us together again."

That's when I noticed that Trahaearn was lying on his side. "Did you use his power?"

"Yes, but he's fine. Look."

Trahaearn groaned and pushed into a sitting position. "What happened?"

Beacon answered, "We aren't sure. Inlackt seemed to be healed and then... well he exploded as we left."

"We need to go back," Dionne said, frantic. "I did something wrong."

"You didn't do anything wrong." I was amazed at what she had accomplished. We'd deal with Inlackt, but she was my apprentice, and that made her my priority.

As we fussed about what to do, Lionel's body arched and a great moan burst from him. I reached for him, knowing that I was responsible for his body even if I couldn't get his soul back into it alone. There was no pulse under my fingers, no heat in the body.

My own heart stopped. What had I allowed to happen? I should have prevented us from making it worse. I heard Dionne call my name seemingly from a great distance. As I gasped in a breath to order Trahaearn to do something, Lionel relaxed, warmth flowed from him, and his heart started beating.

"Thank you for this body," Inlackt said wriggling his shoulders as if he was trying to make a jacket sit better. "It is large, but I have managed to inhabit it, and now I have my magic back too. It is like coming home after a long absence."

We left the basement for the warmer, and drier, kitchen.

Trahaearn stumbled on the top step. "I need a few minutes in the garden. Your workroom is not sufficiently powered to give me what I need," he said, voice shaky. Stripping off his jacket and tee-shirt, he crossed to the back door.

I followed him to make sure that he wasn't observed. The neighborhood was quiet. Lights shone in my neighbor's homes, but it was almost full dark. I guess we're draining the power faster than it could return from the bedrock where we had sent it for Ms. Metcalfe's visit. Too much had happened since then. It felt like months had passed rather than days. It wasn't even enough time for me to feel secure that my sight was really back.

Tamping down my misgivings so I didn't attract bad luck, I left the druid to his rest and went back to join the others. "Dionne, you will have to leave soon."

She slumped as though I had condemned her to a life in prison. "If I take a cab, I can stay longer. If I lived here, I could drink beer and stay in every conversation. Especially the ones that relate to my future." The last was delivered with a hard stare.

Whether she had a point or not, she had to learn to live with the reality of any situation, not just the ones she liked. The experience of being a foster child that she was so fond of using as an example of how she was able to be resilient, wasn't helping. I was convinced that she was more unrelenting than resilient. "Yes, but between now and then we have a prophecy, a druid healing, and two months of school. Now let's concentrate on getting the first hurdle overcome."

I could tell she was looking for allies in the way she glanced at Beacon and Inlackt. Both ignored her. She shrugged as though it didn't matter, but I could tell it did. "Fine, so what's next?"

"Well, we know where two of the six are, we'll need to find the other four and get them together." I glanced over my shoulder to the garden. "Trahaearn says he knows the rite. We may need to gather ingredients while we wait for the others to arrive."

Beacon swallowed most of his beer in one gulp. "So, we're looking for a witch, a couple of wizards and a fairy."

"Olan had some connections," I said. "He found a child in Wales, and a woman in Bolivia. I think we just need to find a fairy and a wizard."

Beacon grunted. "I know a family of pixies living in the park. If Olan isn't around, maybe they can make contact."

Olan wasn't around and hadn't been for a while. "Any ideas how we'll find the last two?" I asked, hoping that someone would just hand us the answer.

"Bud," Dionne said. "Maybe she can get us some information."

"You have a fairy in your control?" Trahaearn's voice overrode my own response. He sounded surprised and a little as though he was going to call us to account for using power over another being.

Dionne laughed, and I had to join her. "You don't know fairies well, do you?" I managed to gasp out.

"No. I don't think they like the weather where I come from, or maybe they are just shy in my neighborhood. Why?"

I nodded to Dionne who answered, "They aren't in anyone's control. It's like trying to deal with a two-year-old. They imagine the world in a way that suits them, and then just act on it." She grinned. "Bud is the leader of the local Rose fairies. Her mother, Princess, told Quinn he owed her a favor because she let him save her life. That's how fairies work."

He raised his bottle in salute. "Then we'll need to tread carefully because we don't want to take on an obligation. But we do need to find at least the location of the fairy."

I told him what we knew about the others, finishing with, "So, the only one we don't know how to find is the wizard."

His time in the garden had refreshed him, bringing color to his skin and a shine to his eyes. "Then we must find this wizard and bring everyone together. Bolivia, Wales, and some unknown locations, we seem to have a very scattered group," Trahaearn said. "It is odd that the prophecy should come about this way. I am of the mind that this prophecy is a series of tests."

Given what The Morrigan had said about the magnitude of the change coming, I was glad of the need for passing a test. The other side of that coin was Dionne's survival. If we didn't find a way to pass whatever was presented to us, she would only have a few years to live. "I supposed we'll have time to gather the ones we know about. It could be a few days to get the woman from Bolivia, but Wales is only an eight-hour flight."

Dionne traced the pattern on her mug. I could see her

working through the problem, trying to find a better solution. Or at least one that she thought was better. "The one in Wales is a child. How will he participate?"

"Real Folk children are different from humans," Beacon answered. "I've been watching them lately in the park, the human ones. Moss said I have to get to know how everyone uses the park I'm guiding. The humans stay young so much longer than our children. A wizard at four is already trained to follow his teacher in fairly complex magic."

Dionne's eyes widened. "I can't even do that."

"You need to stop thinking of yourself as a teenager," Trahaearn said. "Think of yourself as a very tall two-year-old."

She laughed. I sensed a bitterness to the sound, but let it go for now. It was time to figure out our next steps. "We need to be able to contact the ones we know about, and then find the last two, the wizard, and the fairy." I unnecessarily reminded everyone.

Beacon put his bottle in the recycling box. "I'll go talk to the forest folk about contacting the woman and the child. Maybe the imps and the pixies can find the two missing ones."

"Someone can talk to Bud," I said. "I think I should stay here with Inlackt."

The sprite had been sitting quietly on a stool listening to us. Now his head drooped and his chin rested on his chest. "Is Inlackt awake?" I asked.

Beacon touched Lionel's temple. "He is sleeping, just sleeping. Don't worry, Lionel's body is safe."

Dionne helped Beacon to move Inlackt to the couch, where he was less likely to fall over. Beacon tucked a blanket around him. "We could spell him into sleep so you can leave the house without worrying."

"I do not want to sleep," Inlackt said. "I am tired. Please don't put a spell on me and make me sleep. I want to experience this body. You will take it away soon. Put a spell on me to keep me awake." He sounded piteous.

"Can you help us?" I asked.

"I can feel the others. Why doesn't she?" He waved a hand listlessly at Dionne.

She shrugged, and then sat next to Inlackt. "What should I be feeling?"

"I don't know. I know what I feel. Pressure. Five points." He pointed south. "One there." He pointed at Dionne. "You, I feel you when you move. And there, one." He pointed east. "There. That is all the ones you know. I feel two others—"

"Don't tell me," Dionne said. "Let me figure it out."

She closed her eyes and after a minute she slumped. "I don't feel anything."

Inlackt sighed. "You can touch me, and I'll let you see what I feel." He grabbed her wrist and held her away as she reached for him. "Only if you make it so I can be awake while I have this body."

I knew it was an empty threat. He would die if the prophecy didn't come to pass. It wouldn't hurt Lionel if his body was kept alert for a few days. He could sleep all he needed when he was back in there. "I will give you a charm to keep your body awake for three days. We can discuss it after that. You do not want the body to fail while you inhabit it."

A glint of something flashed in his eyes, then he smiled. "That will be sufficient."

I settled for his answer, even though I wanted to tie down whatever had crossed his mind. "Let Dionne see what you see while I get the charm."

He looked at Beacon who nodded. "Yes, you gave me this body. I can trust you, I think." He let Dionne's arm free and leaned toward her. "Feel the others."

The charm I needed was in the workroom. I was reluctant to

leave when Dionne was doing magic. "Beacon, make sure she's safe."

He placed his hand on her shoulder. "I will monitor her."

I hurried to the workroom, grabbed the nutmeg pod, and returned to the living room. Dionne was in the same position as when I'd left. Lionel's eyes were closed, Dionne's open. Trahaearn lounged in the chair, and Beacon knelt next to Dionne. It all looked like a tableau, like they were posing for a painting.

As I watched, Dionne gasped and pulled back.

"I feel them," she said.

"Where is my charm?" Inlackt asked. "You promised."

I passed him the nutmeg pod. "You only need to keep it in your pocket." As much as I wanted to hear what Dionne had learned, I needed to make sure the sprite didn't damage Lionel's body. "I recommend you take a few naps in the time you use it. To do that, you take the nutmeg out and place it near you. A few feet away, and you'll sleep for ten or so minutes. In another room, you'll sleep until you are rested."

"Why would I sleep?"

"Lionel's body needs to rest. If you don't let him, your thoughts will become cloudy."

"Okay. I will take a nap now." He tossed the pod on the coffee table and lay down.

I turned to Dionne who was hunched over and drawing on a sheet of paper. "You know where everyone is?"

"Yes," she said. "I feel it as an itch. When I went into his mind, I suddenly realized what I was feeling, or maybe it got stronger."

She finished drawing and handed me a map. The page contained a rough sketch of the continents. Four stars identified the other members of the six. The two we didn't know about until now were circled. One in Japan, the other in Africa. "Do you know which is the fairy?"

She tapped the African location. "That's the fairy. The one in Japan is our wizard. How are we going to get to them?"

Trahaearn took the paper. "We can reach the wizard through the circle. Let's hope he speaks English. You'll need a fairy to bring the other."

I wondered how we'd get a fairy to come to us from all the way around the world. "I'll talk to Bud. I guess we'll be more than a couple of days before we can make this happen."

"No," Trahaearn said. "We can do it in a day or two at most. There must be a way to bring the prophecy to fruition without all six being in attendance. Think, Quinn. If the prophecy had not been confounded before, the six would have had to travel by sailing ship, or on foot across continents."

"Perhaps that is why it has not yet come to pass," Beacon said. "It is only now that all can easily travel to us."

I glanced at the clock. We would have to send Dionne home in the next half hour. "Trahaearn, how do you know we can do this remotely?"

"I don't. I just think it is only be logical that we can do it."

A gentle snore came from Lionel.

I wanted to rely on the logic, but there was so much at stake. "Let's start by contacting all of them first. Then we might have more information."

"And if that information is not useful?" Trahaearn asked.

"Then we'll deal with it. We need to contact Bud."

Beacon rose. "I'll go find her and ask her to come. Quinn, I will be staying the night. I hope that is acceptable."

Why did I feel like I was losing control of everything? "Yes, you are welcome anytime. Well, I guess as long as you fit in my house."

He stretched. "Moss is starting to make his goodbyes. He has a tree picked out to die under. He'll melt into the earth and feed the roots for a long time."

Dionne reached out a hand. "I'm sorry. It must be hard for you."

He shrugged. "I will miss him, but this is the way we live. Now, don't do anything interesting until I return."

Beacon left, promising he wouldn't get involved with park business that would delay him.

I checked the clock. "Dionne, it's time to go. We'll see you tomorrow, early." I wanted to tell her not to come too early, not to arouse suspicions more than they already were, but I didn't want to embarrass her in front of Trahaearn.

"Quinn, what if I call and tell them I'm staying at a friend's house. They don't care." She cleared the few dishes we'd left on the counter.

My main problem contesting her point, was that I wanted her to stay. That she was right, it would be better if she didn't have to leave all the time. "I can't believe that's true," I said. "You looked like part of the family when we saw you. They must care, if they took you in."

She gritted her teeth but didn't say anything.

I hated that unspoken argument. It would linger like fried fish, if we didn't clear the air. "What? You want to say something. Why don't you just say it?"

She glared at me. "You don't want to hear it. You think they are some kind of saints. But they only take in foster kids for the money. Just because they don't beat me, or abuse me, doesn't mean it's not about the money. As long as they get the last few checks, they will be happy enough. And then they'll take in another kid."

Trahaearn was making his way to the garden, I would thank him later for his discretion. Why did these conversations always get started when there was no time to deal with them? "You seemed to care about you foster brother. Are you sure these feelings aren't because you want to live here?"

She started getting her things together, pulling out her phone to call a taxi. "No. Why do you think Ms. Metcalfe is always harping on my school work? It's because my foster parents don't tell her that I'm away so much. All she has is my marks to tell her what's going on with me."

"Then why do you have to lie to them about being here? If they don't care, why do you stay with them?" I could imagine what it was like to live with people who only tolerated you. I couldn't believe that was true about Dionne. How could anyone not care about her?

She ignored me while she ordered the taxi. It gave me time to absorb what she'd said, time to decide if I believed her.

She ended the call and pulled on her jacket. "The cab will be here in five minutes. I'll be here by three tomorrow, unless you'll be okay for me to skip school." She looked at me, but I shook my head. "And I stay because there's a risk that if I don't, they'll send Ms. Metcalfe after me. And you and Lionel will get in trouble." The words had no passion, no pain.

I didn't like the way she'd turned off the emotions. A witch needed to be in control, but bottling anger, or any negative emotion, could lead to disaster if it broke free during spell work. "Dionne, is it really that bad?"

"No, it's not." She blinked back tears. "I didn't really understand it before. I thought it was because I needed to find out what happened to my parents. But..." She swallowed. "But since I met you and Lionel, it's like I'm part of something. And that made me realize I wasn't really part of that family."

Happy that she'd finally told the truth, I relented and said, "I'm sorry. It won't be for much longer. I promise we'll find a way to move you in here as soon as we can." *Even if I have to put a spell on Ms. Metcalfe for a few months.*

"Thanks." She leaned in and kissed my cheek. "Let's forget this happened, okay?"

"Learn from it, Dionne. Don't try to forget things you experience. Good or bad, they help make you into the person you need to become." I had no time to complete the lecture because a horn honked, and she ran for the door.

15

Trahaearn must have been watching because he came through the kitchen door seconds after Dionne went out the front. "She is a powerful witch," he said. "I could feel her emotions through the walls."

"Yes, and she's a teenager. I live in fear of what she'll do under impulse. She says she understands the risks, but she doesn't act like she cares sometimes." Most of the time, if I was honest.

It was time for Lionel to wake. I still couldn't look at the sleeping body and think of Inlackt. It felt too much like I was tying him closer to the physical body, like he would come to own it. But now we needed to find out what he knew. He might be able to give us more information, or maybe not. I figured it was worth a try. "I understand Dionne not knowing about the other five, but Inlackt might be holding back something we need to know."

"It is worth asking," Trahaearn said.

"I am hungry," the sprite's voice was becoming less like Lionel every time he spoke.

I opened the cupboard to find some crackers. I knew there

was cheese in the fridge. Sprites didn't eat meat, so I would have to go looking for more appropriate food later.

"Join us," I said. "There is beer." Sprites do like a drink.

He crossed the room with an ungainly reel. Perhaps alcohol wasn't the best idea, but I didn't want to take my offer back.

Trahaearn did his thing with the beer bottles. Inlackt took one and after three attempts managed to get it to his mouth. I let him get through half the bottle before I asked, "Can you do anything more than feel the location of the others?"

He swallowed the cracker he'd been eating before answering. "Before, I could. With this body, I am finding my way. My powers are there, but they are muted." He was sounding more lucid as time passed.

"It would help us to have more information."

"Can you feel anything more than just a location?" Trahaearn asked. "A name, or something?"

"Will I be able to go outside this house?" The words were casual, but the way he kept his gaze on the bottle confirmed that he was trying to disarm us into giving him something.

We didn't have time for adventures. Lionel needed to come back. "It depends," I said. "We will not have time before we have to make the prophecy come true. Perhaps when we are done. When we know you are safe, we can go to Banks' or to the park."

"Both would be nice." The wistful tone was meant to make us feel sorry for him; I just felt manipulated.

I looked at Trahaearn, he raised an eyebrow, then grinned. "I suppose that we would have more time for adventures if we had more information."

Inlackt perked up, and I had a pang of regret for taking advantage of his desperation to experience life. Not that much, but a pang.

"In Africa, it is a Rooibos fairy. It's a man fairy. I don't know his name. In Japan, the wizard is old, maybe eight hundred years. Very powerful. He will contact you." Inlackt pointed Lionel's fingers at Trahaearn. "He said to go to the cherry blossom tree in this garden. Tomorrow morning at ten. Now we go to the park?"

"No," Beacon said as he joined us. "Not tonight. We will have a visitor in a few minutes." He looked to me. "Bud is coming."

It had been a few days since Bud had become leader of the Rose fairy tribe. If she was coming herself, that boded well. She would have sent one of the other fairies to tell me no.

"I am here Quinn Larson," Bud piped as she flew in and landed next to me. "You need my help?"

I retrieved the honey and handed her a spoon. "Take what you want."

She scooped a heaping spoonful and licked it delicately, sidling up to Trahaearn. "Who is this person?"

"I am visiting from the south," Trahaearn said. "My name is Trahaearn. You must be Queen Bud."

She sucked the spoon dry and looked at him through narrowed eyes. "There is more to you than just visitor. But I will put that aside for now. May I have more of the honey, Quinn?"

I pushed the jar toward her. "Of course."

She looked into the jar and dipped the spoon. "Now will this foreign fairy be ready for us?" she asked.

I knew there would be a problem. Not only would we have to find a way to contact him, we'd need to get him prepared. "How do you mean, ready? What does he need to know?"

She sighed and spoke slowly as if I was somehow unable to understand the most simple information. "If he knows we are calling then he will be able to come to us. If we have to find him, we will be a long time. Do you have a long time?"

"No," I said. "We will make sure he is ready."

She put the spoon on the counter. "Then we can bring the fairy here. You may give him my name so that he will recognize our call. Let me know when you need us. Thank you for the honey, Quinn Larson. I must go." She flitted out of the room.

When we were alone Trahaearn asked, "How do you plan to make sure he is ready?"

"No idea. Maybe we should check out some old summoning spells. It's really only the fairy we don't know about. Beacon will get the information we need about the other two."

"It will take a little time," Beacon said.

"No," Trahaearn said. "We will not wait to find out if Beacon can help us. If we are asking about the fairy, we need to ask about all three."

WE TOOK TURNS KEEPING INLACKT COMPANY OVERNIGHT, THE sprite refused to sleep again and was starving for information. Trahaearn talked to him about world events, Beacon and I brought him up to date on local gossip. I pulled the dawn shift, so I kept him busy helping to prepare breakfast.

"I could help you with grocery shopping," he offered after tipping the last of the oats into boiling water. "We need food. And beer."

"I think we can do some housekeeping stuff after we contact everyone. How about if we make contact with your fellows, and then we can go to Banks' for lunch. I'll go grocery and beer shopping on the way back."

"Okay, is Beacon going to come with us? Will you cast a glamor? I like looking like humans, it gives me freedom."

He'd been chattering for a couple of hours. It allowed me to relax earlier, but now it was getting on my nerves. "Yes, I'll put a glamor on Beacon, but we still have to be fast. He's getting too big to disguise properly."

"I know," Beacon said coming from my room where he'd been sleeping. "It won't be long before I'm confined to the park. It'll be nice to see everyone in Banks' one more time."

The oatmeal was ready. "Inlackt, go wake Trahaearn. We need to get started on contacting the others."

After a fast breakfast, we trooped down to the basement. Beacon bumped his head on the low beam and Inlackt fussed at him until he was ordered to sit in the center of the floor.

I drew the circle around us before joining the others. "Okay, Inlackt. Maybe you can tell us how you talked to the wizard in Japan."

Inlackt cocked his head. "I thought about him, and he contacted me. His name is Haruto."

If it was that easy, we could be ready to go in a few minutes. "Can you think about the others?" I asked.

"It doesn't work. I have tried. But you can try. Maybe it is because of this body?" He gestured to Lionel's chest. "I am not yet inhabiting it fully."

And he'd better not get ready to inhabit it permanently. "Maybe we can use the magic of the circle to contact them. All of them at once and make arrangements."

Trahaearn slipped his shoes off. "I can reach through the earth. It will take some time, but it's strong enough magic."

"Let's try using my usual spirits first," I said pulling some candy from my pocket. "Beacon will you join us to protect Inlackt?" I meant control, but didn't think Inlackt would be happy to hear it.

"I will. Circle magic isn't really my thing, so don't look to me for help." He settled next to Inlackt, as though proximity would help to protect the sprite.

"Are we ready?" After they all nodded, I threw three candies into the circle and called Ranseed. It was as though he'd been waiting for me. There was very little fanfare of dust whirls and scratching noises.

"Quinn Larson, where is your not Lionel apprentice?"

I rolled my eyes. If I didn't know that spirits were incapable of feeling it, I'd swear he had a crush on Dionne — it was probably a crush on new information, if it was anything. "She is not here."

"Strangers in the circle. You are becoming popular."

I heard Trahaearn chuckle and looked up. Beacon was grinning too. I guess my days of solitary practice were truly in the past. I hated the fact that a spirit was the one to make the point. "We have a request," I said refusing to take the bait.

"I will not be as willing to strike a bargain this time."

I should have known Dionne's victory would bite us in the ass. "If you are unwilling to help, please leave the circle so that we can summon a less spiteful spirit."

The sound of rustling leaves roared through the circle then died out. "I did not say I would not help," Ranseed screamed. "I wish to have a good faith bargain."

I waited until my ears stopped ringing. "Name your price, and we will tell you the favor we need."

"No, what is the favor. I cannot find a fair price without knowing what is required of me."

"Fair enough," I said hating to admit he was right, but knowing that he'd think it gave him an edge. I could use that in negotiation. "We need to contact three people who are spread over the world. We wish to speak to them for a few minutes." I hoped it would be short.

"This I can do. Who are these people?"

"That we will tell you when we have a bargain." I hoped we had enough information for him to be successful.

"Very well," Ranseed said. "I will require knowledge of this strange druid. I will require one favor in the future. I will take these candies in payment of listening to you."

That wasn't a precedent I wanted to set. The candy usually worked as payment for information, although what he did with it, I don't know. If it became the price to enter negotiations, it would become too expensive to deal in the spirit world. "No. The candy will be taken away unless it is part of the price of the connection to these three people."

A small cloud of dust rose quickly then dispersed. "Very smart, Quinn Larson. The price for this favor you ask is this, the candy, which I will take now, the future favor, and three pieces of information about the stranger with the tattoos."

I knew that I would be the one filling the favor, so I had no problem making the promise, but Trahaearn might have some difficulty giving information. I glanced at him. He nodded and mouthed, keep it vague, or at least that's what I thought he said. "Very well, we have a bargain."

Ranseed laughed and the candy disappeared. "Tell me what you need. I am anxious for the information."

I explained that we needed to contact the three people, and what we knew.

"Africa is a large place. I will need something more."

"You will notice a bright light like mine," Inlackt said.

"I see your light; I do not know you. Another stranger. Why did I not see you before?"

Inlackt made to answer, but I held up my hand. "That is not part of the bargain."

A sigh like wind through a field of dry corn stalks preceded his answer. "I will need information to complete this favor. Must we bargain for each question?"

That was a good point. I didn't want to waste time bargaining, but I didn't want to just give Ranseed what he asked. I couldn't trust him to keep his questions to what he needed. "I understand, Ranseed. I will answer one question related to the search. If you need more, we will reopen negotiations."

A breath of foul air filled the circle. "I will need to know the reason you wish to contact these people."

"This is not information we can risk being made public," Trahaearn said before I could stop him engaging in the negotiation.

"How long will you need it to be kept secret?" There was avarice in Ranseed's voice.

"We don't know," I said taking back control. "Will you accept that you will know when it is safe?"

"Will the answer to my question help me know when it is safe?"

How had he known to ask that? Ranseed was getting cannier. "Yes, we believe it will. Now are you ready to do the favor?"

"Yes," he hissed. "Do you wish them to come here into the circle? Or can I carry a message?"

"Into the circle, and we need that to be private."

"The answer to my question?"

"We wish to discuss the prophecy of the six." Truth, but not quite all of it.

"Are they the six?"

His question was so fast that I almost answered before catching myself. "One question was what we agreed. Are you reopening the negotiations?"

"No. Wait."

Within seconds, the voice of a child greeted us. "Hello, is it time?"

I couldn't sense any presence. "Are you alone in the circle?"

"Yes," he said.

I explained what we were doing. "Can you come to us?"

"No, I am not able to leave here. I can come to the circle as you call me. My teacher has freed me from my responsibilities."

Interesting. "Do you know if the prophecy can be completed through a circle?"

"It can, of course. You need to call our names and we will come. You have all six?"

It was odd to speak so openly about what we were doing. "We do. We expect to complete the rite within a few days. What name shall we use for you?"

"I will answer to Dai. I must go. Your spirit is pushing me out."

He left without another word.

"Hello? Hola?" A warm voice called.

"Welcome to my circle," I said. Then we had the same conversation.

"You may summon me with the name, Herminia." Then she was gone.

The circle remained empty for a long time. I didn't want to interrupt Ranseed's search, but we couldn't sit here all day.

"Quinn Larson," his voice came thinly through the circle as if he was far away.

"We are waiting."

"The fairy will not come to the circle. He is worried that he will not be able to leave." His tone made it clear what he thought of cowardly fairies.

"Will you take one of us through?" I asked.

"One question of the new stranger will be enough payment."

I looked at Inlackt and Beacon. "I will answer one question," Inlackt answered. "And I will go into the circle."

"No. We can't afford to lose you." I would not leave Lionel's body empty again.

"It must be him," Beacon said gently. "They must be able to trust each other. They have a connection."

I voiced my fear. "And if he doesn't come back?"

Beacon placed his hand on Lionel's head, the hand almost wrapping around the whole thing. "I will keep a thread."

I looked to Trahaearn and he nodded. "Very well, we have a bargain."

Inlackt went limp. We were left looking at Lionel's body, a familiar dread washing over me. It seemed like an eternity, but eventually he jerked upright. "His name is Tamrat. He will come to Bud's circle."

I almost passed out in relief. For once we didn't have a new list of questions. We had exactly what we needed. "Ranseed, you want payment now, I presume."

"Yes. My first question is to the new person who is, and is not, Lionel. Where is Lionel?"

"He is in the amulet," Inlackt answered.

"Interesting," Ranseed said. I had expected him to demand more details, but he just continued, "Now, three questions for the other stranger."

"No, you asked for three pieces of information, not three questions," I reminded him.

"Yes, that is right." There was less annoyance in his voice than I expected. "Very well, stranger, what information will you give me?"

Trahaearn leaned forward. "I am here to right a wrong. I am searching for my people. I will bring truth to this city." The last rang with a force I wasn't expecting.

"Goodbye, Quinn Larson. I would be grateful for a visit with Lionel when he is returned."

A rush of wind and then we were alone. I cleared the circle.

16

Trahaearn returned from his appointment with the Japanese wizard. He had agreed to come to a circle when we called. I wished everything about this was so easy.

Dionne wouldn't be joining us for another three or four hours. It was time to get Beacon disguised and make good on the promise to let Inlackt see the world, or at least that part of it around my home.

I pulled out a few charms that would reinforce the glamor, making Beacon seem only like a tall human rather than a half a tree. Beacon waved them away. "I can cast it on myself. It works better that way. My magic doesn't fight the spell if it creates the glamor."

I watched as he took a deep breath and closed his eyes. I turned off my true sight to see how he would appear to a human. Beacon shrank into himself and lost the green cast to his skin. The bark texture smoothed out and suddenly a tall red-haired human occupied my living room.

"Lunch at Banks'?" I asked. "Beacon, we don't need you back right away if you have to go to the park. We'll stock up on groceries, and I'll make sure we have something in the fridge for your next visit."

"I do need to update Moss." Beacon turned to Inlackt. "I will be unhappy to hear that you caused problems for Quinn Larson."

"Yes, I will behave in the store," Inlackt said. "I have no wish to attract attention. But it would be better if I could come with you to the park." His last words wheedled.

Beacon shook his head. "No, you must stay with Quinn and Trahaearn until the prophecy. Then we will see about you having some time in the park."

I agreed with him. I couldn't quite rid myself of the suspicion that Inlackt was going to steal Lionel's body. As I grabbed my coat, someone knocked at the front door. I wasn't expecting anyone. I glanced at the back door, but it felt cowardly to try escaping that way. "I'll get rid of whoever it is." I turned to encompass everyone. "Don't come near the door."

When I opened it, I came face to face with Ms. Metcalfe.

"Mr. Larson," she said taking a step forward. "I know you said you were busy, but I thought I would drop by for a look around just in case you had a few moments."

I stepped back enough to let her enter but blocked her from going any further into my home. "I am about to leave for a meeting," I said. "I don't have time to show you around." I spoke loud enough to let the others know what was happening, but not so loud that it would seem rude, I hoped.

"It will only take a moment." She tried to step past me, and I had to move quickly to block her. She gained a few steps and I started to panic. I couldn't let her in to see the strangers in my kitchen. And I couldn't trust that Inlackt would pass for Lionel. And I couldn't remember what I'd done with the wards the last time she was here.

"It really isn't a good time," I said. "Perhaps we can agree on an appointment early next week." We should surely be finished with the prophecy by then, and maybe with Trahaearn's problem.

She stiffened, but I could see that it was automatic. Her face stayed interested and open. "It is within my right to call a surprise inspection of Dionne's workspace."

This was going to call for more than just my usual charm. I reached for a compliance spell in my pocket. Just a little nudge to get her to delay this visit, nothing too strong. I didn't want to mess her up with magic.

"Quinn," Trahaearn rounded the corner into my hall. "I am sorry, but we need to leave in the next five minutes, or we might lose the deal."

"I know," I said. I let the charm go and turned to Ms. Metcalfe. "I hate to insist, but if we don't make this meeting, we may not have a business left to employ Dionne."

She looked Trahaearn up and down. I was glad to notice his tattoos were covered. "Is this gentleman living here?"

"No," Trahaearn answered. "I am staying at the hotel on the corner."

"Very well. I suppose I can't endanger her job by delaying you. Let's say we'll meet next Tuesday, at nine am." She made a note in a small calendar.

"That will be fine," I said, sure that we would be back to what passed for normal around here by then. "I promise we'll be available for as long as you need us to be."

She allowed me to usher her out. I watched her get into her car and drive off before I shut the door and returned to the living room. "That woman is going to screw up something important before Dionne is free of the system."

Trahaearn laughed. "I'm sure that is not true. She cares, and not just about her job." He clapped his hands and rubbed them together. "Now shall we go? I am looking forward to a couple of pints of the dark brew that Mark keeps on tap."

· · ·

BANKS' WAS BUSY WHICH WAS NOT UNUSUAL FOR LUNCH. PEOPLE liked to congregate in the day and keep more serious work for the night. We took a table in the back to allow Inlackt to see everything going on around us. I ordered lunch and a round of drinks before settling in.

"Who are all these people?" Inlackt asked, awed.

I looked around. "I don't know everyone in the city, but these are all Real Folk."

Beacon pointed out a few of the local park citizens. I pointed out a couple of others I knew. Then the back door opened and we were graced with a visit from the sidhe court. Maeve followed two of her male escorts and sat at a table near the door, allowing for a quick return to the court. "That's the sidhe queen," I said. "I'll be back in a moment. I must pay my respects."

"Can I come?" Inlackt asked, starting to rise.

"I think that might be a bad idea." I saw the disappointment drag him down. It was like I'd said no to a puppy. A puppy with Lionel's face. "Let me explain the situation to her, then, if she is willing, I'll introduce you."

His smile made me feel like I'd saved his life. I took my beer to the table with me. "Maeve, it is good to see you."

She blessed me with a smile. "I like to see the outside of my court occasionally. I see you have a visitor."

"Yes. I am sure that he will take some time to meet you while he is here."

She sipped from her glass of pale wine. "And Lionel is with you. He seems... odd somehow. Is he ill?"

With her permission, I cast a privacy spell and told her what had happened in the last couple of days. Everything except the discovery of the vampires. That was Trahaearn's story to tell, not mine. "We have a big task ahead of us."

"And are you here to ask for my help?" Her eyes narrowed. I think the message she was sending was a warning. She owed me for stopping Fionuir's plans, but I was treading on the edge of that debt. And I didn't want to cash in this quickly anyway.

"No. This time I think we have it in hand. Of course, I am counting on you keeping Fionuir out of my way. And to keep the identity of the six confidential." I chuckled to soften my words.

She sipped again. "She is safely tucked away, contemplating her mistakes. I will keep her in contemplation until I am certain she is no longer a danger to me, or my court."

My danger didn't even come into consideration. "Thank you." I knew I should just leave, but my promise to Inlackt was poking my conscience. "I wonder if you would be interested in meeting Inlackt."

She glanced over my shoulder. I followed her gaze to see Inlackt staring at us. "He is eager," she said.

"Well, he has so little time with us." I reminded her that he would have to give up the body when the prophecy was done. "Whatever Beacon can do for him, I doubt he'll be able to come to Banks' when Lionel has the body back."

"I will meet him, but only that. It is disconcerting to see someone inhabit a body that does not belong to them." She smoothed her dress, removing wrinkles I couldn't see.

"It is indeed." A shiver of something ran through me as I looked at Inlackt. He was half rising in his chair, eager to come across the room. It was dangerous to approach Maeve without permission. It was as though he had no care for the fate of the body he inhabited. I beckoned to Inlackt. I knew what she was feeling, but I also held the knowledge that there were far more than just this sprite using borrowed bodies.

As he approached, I rose and presented him. "Queen Maeve, I am pleased to introduce Inlackt, a sprite from the past."

He knelt before her. "Your majesty. You probably don't remember me. I spent some time in your court before... well before."

She closed her eyes. "I seem to remember a sprite with your

name. It is good to know you are still with us. Perhaps we will find time to speak when your task is complete." She rose and her escorts stepped forward. "I must return to the court. It was good to see you, Quinn."

"One more question?" I couldn't suppress my curiosity any longer.

"You may ask," she said.

"I have never seen you in Banks' before. Is there some reason you are ranging outside the court?"

"Yes, Quinn Larson. There are rumors that we only hear hints of in the court. I venture out daily to see what comes my way here. I have learned a great deal in the process." She smiled at me again and followed her escorts through the private door.

17

Dionne arrived a little later than expected, but only a few minutes after we finally ended our shopping expedition. I hoped it was because she'd been at school making up time, but I could wait before we started that conversation. We needed to get the preparation complete, so the prophecy would come to pass, and Dionne wouldn't be in danger of dying, at least for that reason. I was looking forward to a time when I didn't have such a dire to-do list.

"So how long before we're ready?" she asked, heading to the fridge. "Hey, you've stocked up."

I shuddered at the memory of grocery shopping with Inlackt. Imagine a six-foot-tall gangly two-year-old, and you'll have some idea of the situation. Thank the fates that he hadn't had a temper tantrum, but Trahaearn and I had to be vigilant about the contents of our basket. Inlackt had a sweet tooth and no understanding of proportion.

"We need to make sure we have everything ready, but I don't see why we wouldn't conduct the rite now," Trahaearn said. "There aren't that many requirements."

We hadn't discussed it, but he was right. I would be more comfortable when the ceremony was complete, Inlackt was in a permanent home, and we'd dispensed with the vampires. The sooner everyone was out of the amulet, the better.

"So, what do we need?" I hoped it wasn't a repeat of the spell that returned my sight. I'd run out of favors to call on.

Trahaearn looked around the kitchen. "Do you have some paper? It's probably a good idea to write it down so that it can be learned."

I dug a notebook and pencil from the junk drawer. "Are you sure you know this well enough to be successful?"

"The list is not for me, wizard. It is for you. When I spoke to Haruto we reconfirmed our knowledge." Trahaearn was scribbling on the paper as he spoke. I saw him draw an intricate design and list six items beside it.

Dionne watched carefully as Trahaearn started to draw a second diagram. "How did Haruto know what to do?"

He glanced up at her, hand paused in drawing. "He is very old."

She frowned. "If he's so smart, how come he didn't reach out to us?"

"He was not sure that this was the right time for the prophecy to occur. It has almost come to be five times since he was born. It was only when Inlackt returned from the amulet that he knew the six were alive. He was making preparations when I found him."

That didn't make sense. "Wait," I said. "Are you saying that he has survived five failures of the prophecy?"

"Yes. He is looking forward to being released from his obligation. He is old even for a wizard and believes that he is being kept alive until the prophecy happens. Then he will be allowed to age and die at a more normal pace."

The shock of his words made me feel unmoored. If this information was true, what other lies had we believed? "We were told that if the prophecy didn't come to pass each of the six would die within two years"

He raised an eyebrow. "Who told you that?"

"The druids." I realized the problem as the words left my mouth. "Okay, I guess I should put everything they told me on the lies side of the information vault." I wasn't ready to put everything Trahaearn said on the truth side, but he hadn't messed with us — yet.

Dionne twisted her hair into a braid and jumped up from the stool. "Can we analyze this later? I want to meet the others."

Trahaearn pushed the paper toward us. "The two designs are for the circle. The first one is the outer and the second is inside, but must be drawn in the north quadrant. The lines must be as close as possible but must not touch."

I looked at the intricate circles. "Will the others have to draw these as well?"

"They will, but they know how," Inlackt said. "They will have rehearsed the circles many times. Even Dai will know how to do it."

Dionne paled. "I've only drawn simple ones," she said. Then seeming to gather her confidence back around her, she laid the paper on the counter and started moving her hands in tracery of the lines. "I should practice. Do we have time?"

Looking at the drawings, I worried that she wouldn't learn them for weeks. This was high magic. It would take me a couple of hours to get it right. "Does it have to be one of the prophesied? Could you cast the circle, Trahaearn?"

He pointed to the space encompassed by the outer circle. "This I can, but only the prophesied can be inside the inner circle, and it must be drawn from the inside."

I looked at Dionne. "Maybe you'll get your wish. If you can make arrangements to stay, we'll practice until you can cast the inner one. Trahaearn can deal with the outer."

Inlackt cleared Lionel's throat. "I am also one of the six," he said with a heavy load of sarcasm. "Do you think I was untrained?"

I could have done without the attitude, but he had a point. I don't know about Trahaearn, but I didn't see Inlackt when I looked at him. I saw Lionel. And Lionel was not one of the six. It was only when Inlackt moved or spoke that I noticed he wasn't my apprentice. Swearing I would get over that until Lionel returned, I asked, "Were you trained?" I was not going to make assumptions. My habit of just believing things had ended a few minutes ago.

"Yes," he said. "It has been a long time, even without the madness of that place, I need to practice, maybe twice."

I relaxed. We were going to be ready.

"So, I guess we need to gather the others and arrange a time to do this?" Dionne's words were rushed as if taking too much time to say them would have an effect on their meaning. "Do we need this circle to do that?"

Trahaearn pointed to the list. "No, we can talk to them through a regular circle. Before we do, can you put your hands on these items?"

I looked at the list; one ounce each of lavender and sage, six butterfly wings, twelve spider webs, one cup of dirt from a barren garden, three drops of dew. "We'll need to get the dirt from my neighbor's garden. The spiders are going to be very angry when we take more of their webs, but we can get this together without too much delay."

Dionne picked up a bowl and wiped it out. "I'll get the dirt. Mrs. Ramos will be at work, and I can get in and out without being noticed. It'll be good practice of my ability to cast a no-see spell." She dashed out the back door.

I figured the risk was low that anyone would see her. The only neighbor who might be home was old Mr. Walker, and he kept to himself. "How are the others going to get lavender and sage?" I asked. Everything else was common all over the world.

Inlackt looked up from where he was tracing the circles. "Those things will be different for each of the six. The herbs are supposed to be common to the place where they live."

It was weird to get answers to my questions about the prophecy. Up to now, we'd just got vague notions and 'I don't knows'. That made we wonder how the knowledge had been lost in this area. Or if Inlackt really had the answers. "Inlackt, what happened to your teacher?"

He didn't move from his tracing of the pattern. "He died. Why?"

"Was he the only one who knew all of this?"

"Yes," Inlackt said. He finished the last two strokes of his copy of the patterns. "He was taught by his master, who died. If I had not been trapped in the amulet, I would have become the teacher and started training the next candidate."

We really needed a way to keep knowledge like this safe. The druids were supposed to be that place, but there must be a way to do it more safely and more widely. Maybe some kind of computer directory. It was the kind of thing Lionel and Dionne would love to do.

Dionne threw open the back door and slipped in. She peeked out through the curtains before bringing a heaping bowlful of dirt to the counter. "That was close. Mrs. Ramos now has a dog. A big one." She washed her hands and poured a large glass of water. "There are plenty of webs, but I figured we probably need them fresh when we cast the circle."

I grabbed the box of chalk I kept in my room, and we went downstairs. "We'll start with contacting the others, and then Inlackt can practice with this chalk." I placed the box on my workbench. Seeing an objection on Trahaearn's lips, I added, "Don't worry, I have plenty of salt for the real one. I just don't see the value in making a practice circle that might come live by mistake."

Dionne set the regular circle in salt and we took our places. Trahaearn removed his shoes and placed his feet to make sure the tattoos touched earth.

He looked at me. "Your power has risen sufficiently that we can use it for the invitation. Do you want me to check that it is clean?" He must have realized that his words could be taken as offense, because he smiled and added, "I can replenish from the power of the earth. Unless you can do that, we should make sure yours is ready for use in the prophecy spell if needed."

It was sensible, and I could hardly take umbrage at his suggestion that my workspace might be fouled, since we'd been attacked more than once through it. "Go ahead."

He closed his eyes, and I felt the dirt floor warm as his magic flowed. Opening his eyes after a short time, he said, "It is clean."

We settled into comfortable positions. Dionne to my right, Inlackt to my left, and Trahaearn across the circle. We were placed at the cardinal points. Any wizard or witch with minimal training automatically did that, and as little as I knew about druids, I knew they were a type of wizard.

Trahaearn called the names, and one by one their images appeared in the circle. Haruto was a wizened old man dressed in baggy jeans and a Kiss tee shirt. Herminia appeared as a small dust devil. Dai's image was a young boy dressed in a suit, and Tamrat appeared as a small bush.

"Welcome to our circle," Trahaearn said before introducing us.

"It is almost time," Haruto said. "It is good to meet everyone."

"This meeting is to make the arrangements," I said. "We want to ensure everyone has what they need and set a time."

"So much hurry," Herminia said as the dust devil danced around the circle. "Yes, I have what I need. I find I am anxious to do my part. Isn't that interesting? I have never thought of this as a burden, but now I wish to get on with my life."

Inlackt and Dionne reached into the circle as one. They placed their fingers on the dirt and two new images appeared in the dust. Dionne became a bird and Inlackt a small tree.

Tamrat's bush started to bounce. "Who is this one? He feels wrong."

"We need to tell them," Dionne said. "We should have no secrets."

In the short time he'd been with us, I'd become so used to keeping everything about Inlackt secret that I almost said no without thinking. Trahaearn held up his hand to stop Dionne from speaking. "Don't be rash." He addressed the images in the circle, "I can assure you that he is legitimate."

"We do not have to trust your assurances, druid," Dai said with an authority that belied his age.

Dionne and Inlackt were quiet, letting us work out the best resolution. The only reason we needed to keep this a secret was to keep the local druids, damn no, vampires, from finding out that we knew what they had done. Not wanting to argue this longer, I said, "No, we can tell them."

"Very well," Trahaearn said. "This information is confidential."

"Who would we tell?" Herminia laughed. "Your area of the world is not that important."

I gave them the details of Inlackt and Lionel's history. "So, you see we have reason to move quickly."

Haruto was the first to react. "I can come to you if you require help. This is not something you should undertake blindly. With your only trained participant in such... odd condition, it may be dangerous for you."

"We are sufficiently prepared," I said, hoping it was true. "If we can gather everyone and complete the prophecy rite, we can restore the balance to the druids."

"Yes, I agree that we should proceed. We are all ready to go on with our lives," Tamrat said. "So, when will we do this?"

"Within the hour if you are ready," Trahaearn said.

I felt the level of tension increase — tension and excitement.

"You will need to call one of us to be there," Haruto said. "Three must come together."

I glanced at Trahaearn. He'd been wrong about the ceremony, was it possible he was wrong about the druids? "We don't know a lot about the ceremony," I said.

Trahaearn leaned toward the center. "This is what I know." He listed the ingredients. The others agreed. "And my understanding is that not all of the six need to be together."

"No," Haruto said. "Three need to be in physical contact."

"That is what I was taught," Herminia agreed.

"Yes." The answer came from Tamrat and Dai at the same time.

"Okay," I said. "It's not a problem."

"How can it not be a problem?" Herminia asked. "Are you suddenly in less hurry to deal with your vampires?"

I didn't care for the way she interrupted me, but I kept that to myself. "If Tamrat is still willing, we can bring him here."

"I can come to visit?" He sounded excited, and I worried about his ability to be serious for the ceremony. I hoped that all fairies were like ours. Able to be frivolous and focused. "I am ready. What will I need to do?" The small bush danced around the circle, making me laugh and feel a little more optimistic. I guess fairies were fairies no matter how serious the situation.

Trahaearn was grinning. "Yes, we can arrange for you to come. You will be called by the fairies so that your power will still be whole when you get here."

"When? I have to gather my ingredients. Who is going to call me?"

We could take care of part of the problem. "Bring only your local herbs. We will supply the others. You will receive a call from the queen of the Rose fairies."

"I will be ready in a few minutes. I must tell my family that I will be going." The dust forming the image of a bush collapsed back into the earth.

"This will be interesting," Herminia said. "When do you need us to be ready?"

"In one hour," Trahaearn said. "We should have everything in place, and it will give us a chance to practice the rite again. We will call you to the circle of six."

Each of them said goodbye and let their image collapse back into the dirt of the floor.

I stretched and broke the circle protecting us. "Dionne, clear the salt with the spell you learned from Lionel. When that's done, help Inlackt use the chalk to practice the one we need for the ceremony."

This time she didn't argue, she just closed her eyes and started muttering the spell. The salt shimmered and lifted from the soil. I didn't wait to see if she was able to collect it into the bowl. There would be time to check when we made sure the soil was pristine for the ceremony. "Trahaearn, come join me upstairs."

When we were alone, I started with my questions. "I guess we'll need to supply the ingredients for Dionne, Inlackt, and Tamrat."

"Other than the herbs for the fairy, yes." He looked at the dirt.

I tried to keep my fear out of my voice as I asked, "Are you sure you haven't missed anything important. Like the ceremonial circle?"

He didn't answer for a moment. It felt like he was angry at my accusation, but it could have been just concentration. "You knew nothing until I arrived. How will we know if I have holes in my knowledge?" So, anger then.

I didn't take the bait. Arguing wouldn't help. And I had no argument against his question anyway. "I'm just worried. If we get this wrong, we could cause some major damage."

"I am not used to getting things wrong, wizard." He snapped at me and then stopped. He held his head in his hands and rubbed at his scalp before looking up at me again. A grin on his face, he said, "I apologize. You have every right to question my information. I have been doing the same myself. Without access to my library, I have nothing to fall back on but my memory."

As much as I dreaded getting something wrong, I knew we wouldn't be effective if we carried this doubt into the ceremony. "I don't think there's anything important you can get wrong now. The others confirmed everything. Perhaps I am too used to mistrusting druids."

He nodded, but his attention was outside, in the garden or something. "Is your neighbor likely to be home?"

I glanced at the sky. The sun was still high above the rooftops. "Not yet, but soon. Can you get more of the dirt, and gather the webs?"

He stood and went to the kitchen. "You have enough of the other ingredients?"

I grabbed my coat before answering. "Yes, that's not a problem. I'll go talk to Bud. She'll find a way to sneak Tamrat to us. It will be tricky because it won't be dark, and she's terrified of humans. But she will find a way."

He took two cups from the cupboard. "I'll check on the circle when they are done. I think we need to make sure everyone has some food in them. I'm not sure how long this will take, but it will take power."

A tremor of excitement ran through my bones. We were really that close to the prophecy. I shrugged into the coat and said, "It feels like we are on a train that isn't going to pull in at any station we know."

He was still distracted, anxious to get outside and feel the earth beneath him, I guessed. He glanced at me before reaching for the back door. "I'm sure it will work out, Quinn. Even if it's a problem, we'll find a way to deal with it."

I tried to take on a little of his confidence, but all I could feel was tension, and a deep fear that we were about to embark on a dangerous journey.

Bud was ready for me and assured me she would have Tamrat at my house before we needed him. "Leave the window to your kitchen open, Quinn Larson. We will get him through there."

As I walked through the park toward the street, I tried to imagine what the world might look like when the prophecy was done. A great change was all we knew. The others didn't have any more information.

I cast my mind back to the last time I'd dealt with prophecies. It was maybe sixty years ago. And the prophecy wasn't so secret. We all knew what to expect. The sidhe were involved, and Mark. It had been odd to see the two extremes working together. The delicate sidhe with their ornate clothes and manners, with Mark, a troll who could have passed for a rock if he sat quietly.

The balance of power had changed. Until then, the sidhe had some power over the other Real Folk. Not much, but it meant they were often the judge and jury in disputes. Since then, we'd all been loosely associated but independent. And there were far fewer disputes.

"Be careful, Quinn." The warning brought me up short. I was about to leave the park and step onto the street. I looked around, but couldn't see who had spoken. The voice sounded like Moss, but there was no way he could hide from me here. The largest plant was an ancient rhododendron, and that only stood about five feet tall.

"I'm here." It was definitely Moss. "Look down, wizard."

I looked lower to the ground and saw a miniature Moss leaning against the trunk of an Arbutus sapling. "Wow, I heard you were going, but I had no idea."

"I'll be gone by morning." He didn't sound sad or regretful, or any emotion I would expect. sprites are very different from other creatures. The whole dust to dust was pretty literal for them.

I would be sad, but I knew it was natural. "Are you going to the ground, or a tree?"

He shrugged. "Haven't decided. I hear the prophecy of the six is about to come to pass."

"Yes, you'll live to see the change." I moved closer, not wanting to be overheard, and worried as much about my paranoia as I was about any spies. When had I become so fearful? "I'll miss you, but you've done a good job with Beacon."

"I know. I'm glad I was able to talk to you first. I would ask that you check in on Beacon. At least for the first little while." He looked unconcerned despite his words. It must be hard to let go control after so many years tending the creatures and plants of the park.

"Of course. He's my friend. I would do that anyway."

A small frown crossed his face. "I have this feeling that he will have to overcome challenges I never did. It will be good to know you will help him. I will erase all your debt for that favor."

Being free of debt to Moss felt great, although I didn't think that he'd erased the debt. My being there for Beacon was payment. "It will all work out fine, Moss." I heard Trahaearn's words echo through mine.

"I know." Moss pushed off the trunk and shook my hand. "I have other goodbyes to make. Beacon will come back to help with Inlackt, but it will be the last time he will leave the park."

I watched him wander deeper into the trees before I returned home. When I walked through the door, I heard voices chattering happily in the kitchen. I hung up my coat and headed in.

"Great, you're back," Dionne said. "I've made sandwiches and Trahaearn says we have the circle right. You can check the purity of the workspace, and then we just have to wait for Tamrat." She was bursting with energy. I had barely sat down before she placed a plate in front of me.

"Open the kitchen window," I said reaching for a sandwich. "Tamrat should be here soon."

My conversation with Moss had dampened my enthusiasm, but Dionne was bringing it back. And perhaps the food. I'd been right to make sure we were fueled for this ceremony. Low blood sugar can make the difference between success and disaster.

And that's the last time I would think about us failing. I was becoming the gloomy old wizard that I feared in my youth.

18

A few minutes later there was a tap at the open window and Bud's head appeared. "Are you ready," she whispered.

I went to the door and opened it. "No need to come through the window," I said beckoning them in.

"No, I will go, Quinn Larson. Come and get me when Tamrat wants to go home." She pushed her companion through the door and scurried to the closest bush.

Tamrat turned out to be a dusty fairy, about three feet tall including a bushy mass of bright yellow hair. His wings were fully extended and quivering.

"Come in," I said. "Dionne, get the honey out, please." I hoped his shivering was to do with hunger rather than blinding fear.

"Thank you. It is very cold here," he said. "Oh, here are my ingredients. Rooibos seeds and bitter melon rind."

I took them and added his few pieces to the tray holding ours. He had brought only a few seeds and a half inch square of rind. We had possibly gone overboard with the amount that we had collected, but it was what Trahaearn had listed.

Dionne opened the honey jar and handed Tamrat a spoon. "Take what you need. We have plenty."

We watched as he made quick work of three spoonfuls. "Thank you for your hospitality. I am ready when you are." He looked around. "Will you all be in the circle? It will have to be very large."

Inlackt held out his hand. "We can draw a very large circle. Come, I think we need to start now."

Downstairs, Inlackt had us all stand in the center of the dirt floor while he took the salt and knelt with his back to us. He used a trickle of salt to build the intricate outer circle, moving a few inches at a time. I was impressed, and more than relieved, at his ability to focus on one thing for so long. When the circle was complete, he asked Tamrat and Trahaearn to verify that he had it right.

They walked side by side, Tamrat tracing the pattern in the air and nodding every few steps. "It is perfect," the fairy announced. "I am very glad I did not have to write it so large."

"Now, we separate," Inlackt said. "Dionne and Tamrat, join me here. I'll create the inner circle and then we can start."

Dionne put the tray of ingredients in the center of what would be the inner circle. She stepped back to me. "Don't worry. We'll be fine."

I pulled her into a hug. If this went wrong, I wanted her to remember that she was loved. We might fight about her time and her behavior, but I didn't want to lose her. I'd had enough of loss. "We'll all be back together soon, and then we'll get you ready to be a witch. I know you can do this."

She squeezed me and then let me go.

Tamrat and Inlackt were watching us. "Come on, Dionne. It will only take a few minutes," Tamrat said.

I motioned for Trahaearn to sit beside me, thinking we were less likely to react badly if we sat. "I thought this might take hours."

"I had no idea how long it would take." He shifted. "It feels weird not to be in contact with the ground."

He'd kept his shoes on this time, and I saw that he was wearing gloves. He noticed my glance. "If my skin touches the earth, my power affects it. I don't think we want that to happen right now."

"Good point." I turned my attention to the inner circle. There was a very faint shimmer of power between the three in the center and us. I could see perfectly, and I could hear them calling the other three. I hugged my arms around me to avoid reaching out to help. This was going to be a hard few minutes.

They joined hands, alternating between a physical entity and a projected image. When they were linked, the three who were images, solidified. They were still images, but they were denser. It was like watching someone come into focus through fog.

As we watched, they laid the spider webs out to form a covering on the earth. Haruto, Herminia, and Dai's webs transformed from dust images to real webs as they came into contact with the ones from my garden.

They were talking, but all six voices blended into one sound. I couldn't make out the words. I guess it didn't matter. We wouldn't need them in the future. I wasn't the only one struggling with being outside the circle. Trahaearn was vibrating with some need. Probably having something like this unfold in front of him was as hard to just watch as it was gratifying to witness.

"I think they are building a world of sorts," Trahaearn muttered. "See the webs are the base; butterfly wings are now covering the webs."

He was right, the dirt covered the wings, and then they sprinkled the seeds across the resulting mat. After a few minutes of chanting that I couldn't understand, they each sprinkled tears on the mat.

Starting with Inlackt, each of the six took hold of the mat and they folded it into a square, without lifting the whole mass from the ground. As soon the last corner was created, all six leapt onto it and started to smash it into powder. When their creation was only a loose scattering on the floor of my workroom, the six bowed to each other and suddenly there were only three.

Tamrat wiped a gap in the inner circle and they stepped out. A foul odor of rot and blood followed them.

"It's done," Inlackt said. "I don't know what it means, but it's done. Now can I go to the park?"

Dionne cleared the outer circle, which also removed the stench from the spell. "I'm a bit wiped out," she said.

"I'm..." Inlackt folded in on himself and hit the ground.

I rushed forward, terrified of finding him lifeless. If he was dead, what would happen to Lionel? Dionne beat me to the body. She placed a finger on his neck and sighed. "He's passed out. He should have rested more before the ceremony. I think we all need to sleep for a while."

Trahaearn lifted Lionel's body and deposited him on the couch. I told Dionne to sleep in Lionel's bed. Tamrat was shaky on his feet but said a few spoonfuls of honey would be enough to revive him. He was correct, two spoonfuls of honey and he was ready to go back to the park. "I can't get Bud yet," I said, thinking it could be a couple of hours before I could head to the park to arrange for her to come.

"Oh, I'll just call her," he said. Then, putting his fingers between his lips, he blew, but I heard nothing.

Feeling relief that at least one of the major problems on my list was solved, I pulled two beers from the fridge. "I think we can risk a drink before we send Inlackt back. I know I need one."

Trahaearn popped the cap and took a long drink. "It does feel a bit anticlimactic. I guess we should be grateful we haven't been invaded by flying monkeys. Or maybe they are on their way."

I resisted the urge to look out the window. "Yes, I guess subtle is better than apocalyptic." My next sip was interrupted by a scratch at the back door. Bud was ready to take Tamrat back.

"Is it done, Quinn Larson?" she asked. "Is the time of the fairies starting?"

I beckoned her in. "What makes you think that the prophecy is about the fairies ruling the world?"

"Perhaps think is a strong word. I hoped," she said. "But what happened?"

Tamrat took one last lick of the honey. "We don't know. I would like to go home, I think. Perhaps it is not a good time to visit. It is very cold in this part of the world."

Bud slid a glance to the honey jar and then sighed. "I will visit in a few days, Quinn Larson. Beacon said to tell you that he will be here when it is dark."

They crept through the open door, and I watched them hurry through the garden to the rhododendron before shutting out the world. "It will be dark in an hour or so. How long before we go back to the amulet to get Lionel, so we can free the druid souls?"

"If Dionne is up to it, we can do it in a couple of hours," he said. "I am anxious to move on the vampires, but not at the expense of your apprentice. Inlackt won't have to do anything, but Dionne will need to be with us in the amulet."

I'd been hoping to let her rest longer than that. I hated the idea of sending her home late and worn to a thread. "You don't think we can find Lionel ourselves?" There was something about the way we had left him that made me wonder if he would be able to stay at the portal, or whatever it was that allowed us entry, for long.

Trahaearn shook his head. "They are connected somehow. He seems more willing to come to her when she calls him. If there is a problem, we will need her there."

As much as I didn't want to put her in danger, now that she was simply an apprentice, he was right. "Okay, let's get some food ready for when they wake."

Trahaearn joined me in the kitchen and started pulling ingredients from the fridge and cupboards. "Let's do something a bit more interesting than your usual stew or porridge."

Was he trying to say I couldn't take care of my apprentices? "That's about all I can manage. Lionel isn't better. Maybe Dionne will show a talent." I hoped we didn't need to wait until she woke up.

"Sit and have another beer." He nudged me out of the kitchen. "I can cook."

He placed a chicken on the counter and added a stack of greens that I hadn't remembered buying, along with a handful of potatoes. I guess Inlackt wasn't the only one adding stuff to the basket when we shopped.

"The grove kitchen was my responsibility before I became arch druid," he said, turning on the oven. "I still like to prepare a meal. It's good you have an apprentice to clean up after we're done. I never got to like that part."

"Tell me about your grove," I said. It was bugging me that I had been so fooled by the vampires. When we cleared up that mess, I was going to keep an eye on the druids to make sure no one attacked them again. At least until they recovered.

Trahaearn mixed some herbs into a blob of butter. His focus on the cooking, he didn't look up when he spoke, "A druid grove is a place of great knowledge." He slid the butter under the skin of the chicken, which was sitting in a roasting pan. The pan went into the oven. "We hold and share knowledge for everyone within reach of our grove."

As he prepared the meal, and the aroma of roasting chicken flowed through the house, he shared his story.

"My parents were surprised when I said I wanted to go to the grove. The family hadn't produced a scholar in generations. But we druids are different from other wizards. We crave knowledge, and we live to teach."

"That does sound familiar," I said. "But the local druids seemed to be all promise and no delivery."

He washed the potatoes under the tap and glanced at me. I saw something in his eyes, maybe suspicion. Taking a paper towel, he dried the potatoes and cut them into quarters. He must have made a decision because he started talking as he worked. "The vampires would not pass close observation. The way of druids is secret, so they would not have been able to access the information should anyone request it." He tossed the potatoes into the roasting pan and started to clean the greens.

Lionel would be happy to know he could research to his heart's content when he returned. Although perhaps I shouldn't assume Trahaearn would be willing to allow the training when we were done. "How do you know when a wizard is truly a druid? I mean we all like to gather spells and bits of information."

He dried his hands. "There is a test. Are you thinking of Lionel?"

I nodded. "He was eager to visit the museum and spend time researching."

Trahaearn placed a pot of water on the stove but didn't turn the element on. "Do you have a compost?" he asked pointing to the pile of stems and peels on the counter.

"Put it in the bucket. Dionne will take it out later."

He joined me at the counter, bringing two beers with him. "I don't think Lionel is a druid. He is too self-sacrificing. You may have noticed that we are an arrogant group."

I chose not to comment on that. "When we're done," I said. "How will you make sure the grove is set up correctly?"

He glanced at me sideways, and I got the feeling I was close to a line that he'd drawn. "That will depend on the state of the souls. Why do you ask?"

Something had slipped off the conversational plane, and I felt like I had to defend my words. "I was wondering what we could do to help. It seems only right that we help." I hoped that he couldn't tell I was babbling to cover a lie.

I must have been convincing because he lost the suspicion in his eyes. "It will depend. If the head of the grove is sane, he will take control. If not, I may have to appoint someone until I can find a new head."

This was something that made him touchy, and until we had finished our tasks, I didn't want to risk losing his friendship. "That smells good. How long until it's ready?"

"Forty-five minutes give or take." He stretched. "I think I need to wash. Would you mind if I took a shower?"

I told him where to find the clean towels and decided to relieve Dionne of her scullery duties by clearing the mess he'd left.

In the garden, I tipped the garbage onto the compost pile and stood watching the sun drop behind the neighboring roofs. It would be full dark soon. There was still nothing different about the world. Nothing felt different about me. So much for great change being brought about.

19

I put the compost bucket back in its place beside the back door and decided one more beer wouldn't hurt. Before I could open the bottle, someone knocked at the front door. Maybe it was Beacon, although I wasn't expecting him for at least another hour.

I opened the door and took a step back. Ms. Metcalfe. Her face was drawn and there were deep lines beside her mouth. She wasn't a young woman, but she wasn't aged either.

"Mr. Larson. May I come in?" she asked, voice shaky. "I'm afraid that there may be some bad news."

I couldn't say no since she looked about to cry. "Please, come into the kitchen and tell me what's wrong."

She followed me down the hall and dropped her briefcase on the floor as though it weighed too much for her.

I fingered a charm in my pocket and released the spell that would keep Dionne and Inlackt where they were and lock the doors. I heard the water running in the shower, but let Trahaearn have his freedom. If he wandered out naked, maybe Ms. Metcalfe would cheer up.

"Can I offer you some tea?" My usual method of entertaining

people I would prefer would leave. This time I meant the offer. I could give her a tea blended specifically to settle her nerves.

"No, I can't stay too long. I'm looking for Dionne. She was supposed to meet her counselor after school and didn't show up. He only thought to report her absence at the end of the day."

It was obviously a losing battle to get Dionne to stop taking risks. I couldn't say it was wrong for her to duck out of the appointment, but I would have liked to know. "Perhaps she is with friends?"

"So, she isn't here?" Ms. Metcalfe tilted her head toward the sound of the shower. Suspicion warring with exhaustion on her face. It looked like exhaustion won as her whole body drooped.

"No, we haven't seen her." I decide that a bold lie was the only way to go. "I wasn't expecting her today. Is this your first stop?"

"No." Ms. Metcalfe rubbed her temples. "I contacted her foster parents, but they don't expect her home until much later. They weren't clear on where they expected her to be. And I am very disappointed that they would allow her to be out late on a school night."

I didn't know what to say to that.

She continued, oblivious to my silence, "At that age, they are so hard to handle. It's when even the best foster parents give up. It takes a lot out of them."

She'd run out of words, so I ventured, "Dionne is a smart girl. I'm sure she will be fine. And I'm not sure anyone could keep her from doing anything she wanted to do."

"Yes, she's headstrong. But things working out for the better is not my experience. There are so many people out there trying to take advantage of young girls." She wiped her eyes.

The shower had stopped while she said that last bit. I hoped Trahaearn had the sense to put on some clothes, the thought of her seeing him naked wasn't so funny in the face of her distress. "If I hear from her, I'll be sure to let you know," I said. "I'm afraid this is the last place Dionne will come."

"But she loved this job."

"That's true." I had to completely drop my ban on lying. Whatever happened, we needed Dionne free of this system, and so a few fibs couldn't make it any worse. "In the last couple of time she worked here, we had some arguments."

"I'm sorry to hear that," Ms. Metcalfe said. "Teenagers can be so changeable."

"Yes. She did a great job, but then she seemed to think she knew better than I did how the business should be run." I resisted the urge to add a little magic to encourage her to believe. I'd told Dionne that it was too risky to interfere with human will, and it was. Besides she was believing me without any urging from magic.

Ms. Metcalfe started to gather her purse. "I must go. There are other places I can look. I can visit her friends."

"Quinn?" Trahaearn joined us, fully dressed. "Is that Dionne? Oh, Ms. Metcalfe."

She stopped getting ready to leave. "You are still here." Her eyes took in his appearance, but she didn't seem to care that he was damp from the shower.

"Yes, I should have been gone, but Quinn needed my help. Dionne seems to have abandoned us."

She sighed and drooped a little more. "Well, I'll be going. Please call me if she contacts you."

"Is it possible that she has run away?" Trahaearn asked.

I really didn't want to make Ms. Metcalfe any more upset. I glared at Trahaearn from my position behind her. "I'm sure she'll show up soon. Dionne is levelheaded even though she's been moody lately."

She pulled her coat around her, regaining her authority with the movement. "I don't know, Mr. Larson. Over the years, I've had a few girls run away in the last few months of care. One of them got married, and I'm glad to say she is still with her husband and very happy. Two or three met up with the wrong kind of man. And a few I never heard from again." She stopped preparing to leave. "I shouldn't get so involved, but I can't help it."

"You need to rest for a few minutes. I'll make that tea." I took her coat and hung it up. "I won't take no for an answer."

Trahaearn joined me in the kitchen. "You'll be putting some skullcap in the tea?" he whispered.

I nodded and worked a charm that kept our voices confined to the kitchen. "Don't upset her even more. If we can get her out of here, we can get back to work. If we don't settle her down, and convince her that Dionne is safe, she won't leave us alone."

"Dionne told me that this woman liked you. If you want her to go away, you need to be less kind." He looked over my shoulder at her. "My advice is to give her the skullcap tea, and make it strong, so she'll calm down and go on her way."

This was my house and my problem. Trahaearn had been helpful with the prophecy, but that didn't give him the right to take over my life. "I'll calm her down. Don't make it worse by suggesting Dionne is in danger." I ignored the comment that she was attracted to me. I couldn't do anything about that.

"If she thinks Dionne is gone, then she'll be gone. I've dealt with bureaucrats before. They are overworked, and that means they don't push too hard if there's resistance." He seemed too insistent. I would have to get him to tell me his history with bureaucracy when we had time. Most Real Folk have no connection with it at all. Until Dionne came into our lives, my only experience was with buying the house.

I glanced at Ms. Metcalfe. She was on the couch focused on something she held below my line of sight. "She's different. She really seems to care."

"I guarantee she'll be out of your life if you convince her that Dionne's run away." He glanced at the dose of skullcap that I'd measured out and shook his head.

Irritated at his pushiness, I snapped the lid on the tin so he couldn't add enough to put her in a coma. "I'll take care of it. Why don't you go to my room and wait until she's gone?"

He shrugged and left us alone. I mixed a blend of chamomile and skullcap with black tea, heavy on the tea. She'd be relaxed and able to rest, and safe to drive her car. I reached for the jar of charms and found one that would help increase the effect of the herbs in a more controlled way. I activated the spell and placed it next to the pot while the tea steeped. "Would you like honey, or sugar?" I called to her.

She looked up from whatever she was doing and said, "I don't take sweetener thank you."

That would leave the tea tasting bitter. "You look like you need the energy boost. Perhaps a little honey?"

She agreed, and I brought everything to the living room where she was still looking at something in her lap. When I placed the tray on the coffee table, I noticed she was texting.

It made me worry that someone would point her back in our direction. "Have you found someone who has seen Dionne?"

She looked up. "No. I'm afraid your friend is right. She's found someone who has offered her a dream of a future, and that's the last we'll hear from her."

I was determined to make sure that wasn't the case. Dionne was going to send Ms. Metcalfe a message as soon as she turned eighteen. She'd come up with a story that would make this woman feel like she'd been successful. Despite what Trahaearn thought, this was one bureaucrat who cared about more than just the appearance of doing her job. "Drink your tea. You'll feel better."

I could feel her tension drain away as the herbs did their work. "It is pretty late, Ms. Metcalfe. Perhaps you should just go home and start looking again tomorrow. Maybe she'll call." I was getting nervous that Beacon would be knocking on the door before she went. Then I would have to admit, even if just to myself, that Trahaearn was right.

"Yes, I do tend to get too involved. My supervisor is always telling me to maintain my emotional distance. He thinks it will help me do a better job." As she spoke the tightness left her shoulders and her posture improved, as though she now had the energy to hold herself upright.

"It must be difficult to keep distance when you are working with kids." I dug deep for the sympathy she seemed to need. Even knowing she had to go soon, I couldn't bring myself to be rude.

She took a last sip of the tea, and placed the cup back in its saucer with a care that made me worry I'd overdone the skullcap. "I do need to get going, Mr. Larson. I'll take it up in the morning. I think perhaps I've gotten too deep with this." She sounded much calmer than when she had come in, and not overly sedated.

"Good," I said. "Let me know if you hear from Dionne. I am also worried about her." Where had that come from? I wanted this woman out of our lives not obliged to give us updates.

"You are a kind man, Mr. Larson." She pulled on her coat and slung her bag over her shoulder. "I must say that getting your sight back seems to have boosted you. You have a healthy glow." She blushed. "Oh, look at me, getting silly. I do really need to get a good night's sleep."

I tried to keep my face from showing my discomfort. If she was going to get more open with this attraction, I was going to have to be more clear that I didn't share it. I hated the thought. There was a time, not so long ago, when I was alone. And I remember being happy, no apprentice, no interference, no prophecy, no vampires. Now I seemed to attract entanglements. "Goodnight. I will let you know if Dionne calls." I opened my front door and waited for her to pass through.

"Thank you for the tea," she said.

I didn't know what to do to make her actually go. I needed to get the human influence out of my life and get back to the familiar magical folk. And she needed to be gone before Beacon arrived, there was no way I could explain a seven-foot-tall sprite, even if he had found a way to minimize his size. With Moss gone,

Beacon wouldn't be able to pass for a human any longer because his growth would be more rapid until he reached full height, maybe twenty feet or more.

I said goodnight again, and she seemed to take the hint because she made her way down the steps and across the street. Relieved, I checked that the street was empty and closed the door on the world.

20

As I made my way back to the kitchen, I released the lock spell on the bedrooms and basement. Dionne immediately joined us in the living room. "I heard everything. Does this mean I can stay here? I mean, I can't exactly go home without a good story, right?"

I held up my hand. "Not now. Trahaearn, can you check on Inlackt? We'll need to get Lionel back and do something with Inlackt before morning."

He nodded and left. Perhaps I just needed to be more directive. No one argued when I told them, so maybe I would just keep telling them what to do, instead of asking. "Dionne, you have to stay in the house until we figure out what to do. I don't want Ms. Metcalfe to bump into you on the street."

The glow in her eyes didn't fade with my words. She looked like someone who was freed from a long and difficult confinement. "Yes, that makes sense."

Trahaearn joined us. "Inlackt will be up in a second."

"Okay. It's almost full dark, so Beacon will be here soon. If we are lucky, we'll get Lionel back before morning."

"Quinn," Dionne said.

Impatient, I responded, "You are going to stay, Dionne. We'll work out the details later."

"No. I mean, thanks, but that's not what I was going to say." There was rebellion just below the excitement of being allowed to move in with us.

Trahaearn stepped into the kitchen, giving us space. I realized just ordering people around wasn't the right thing. I needed to listen too. "Okay. What were you going to say?"

She stepped toward me. "Ms. M said you looked really healthy. You are kind of glowing. Not much, but you are definitely glowing."

I turned to see if Trahaearn was glowing. He wasn't. "What do you mean?"

"Check it out," she said pointing to the bathroom.

She followed me in and stood behind me as I looked in the mirror. She was right, it was faint, but I glowed.

"Is it just me?" I looked at Dionne's reflection and realized I didn't need an answer. "Yes, it's just me." My stomach dropped. I had just got my sight back, now I had some disease that would confine me to my home, because no human was going to miss the glow. Great! Dionne obtains freedom and I get sentenced to house arrest.

We went back to the living room. Trahaearn had pulled the chicken out of the oven. "It's ready. The veg will take a few more minutes." He turned the heat on under the pot and then opened the fridge. "Beer?"

"Good idea," I said. "Let's pretend everything is normal, and we're having a dinner with our friends, and forget we have so much more to do."

"Can I have a beer?" Dionne asked.

"No," I said.

"It might be better for you to wait until we have all our tasks compete," Trahaearn added.

"Fine."

Trahaearn popped the tops of the bottles with his usual magic.

"Whoa," Dionne said. "Check it out."

I didn't need her prompt. Trahaearn was glowing. It started as a bright orange glow that emanated from his entire body. Then it faded until it seemed like an optical illusion.

This was not going to be good. "I think I know what change the prophecy brought. And it's bad for us," I said.

Trahaearn looked at his arm. "This is going to expose us to the humans." It was the first time I'd heard anything resembling fear in his voice.

"No kidding," Dionne said. "What do we do?"

He started pulling plates from the cupboard. "First we eat."

"We'll need to warn everyone to stop doing magic until we can figure out a solution," I said.

The light from the street was dimmed suddenly, then it came back. A few seconds later, someone knocked at the door. Dionne ran to open it. "It's Beacon," she called.

He joined us in the living room. I could see his glamor slip away. "Moss is gone," he said. "I can't stay long. There's some problem with the park."

I realized that most of the folk in the park wouldn't be able to stop doing magic. Mainly because they were magic. I told him what we'd learned about the prophecy.

"I'll get everyone into the deepest areas, but it won't be long before we get found." He flicked a glance at the garden. "I need to do that now."

"You are already starting to glow. You can't set your own glamor," Dionne said. "I'll do it since I can't go out. Be quick, okay? Lionel needs to be free."

Beacon stood while Dionne turned him into a tall homeless person. "I've added a stink so people will stay away."

"Is it safe?" he asked.

I turned off my real sight and there was a faint shine to him, but it faded as I watched. "Yes, you should be fine. We'll do the same to get you back after we return Inlackt to the amulet."

"I have an idea about that... it can wait." Beacon shuffled to the door and left us. I was impressed at the way he got into character so fast.

"Eat!" Trahaearn said. "Until he's back we can't do anything but get our strength up. Where did Inlackt get to?"

Dionne ran down to the workroom, and a few seconds later I heard her arguing with Inlackt. "No, you can't go out right now."

"Why? You all promised I could see the world before I went back." The whine was firmly back in his voice.

She pushed him into the room with frantic motions. "Tell him, Quinn. Tell him what happened. He can't seem to understand."

Inlackt was putting off a light so bright we could have read by it. "Have you been doing magic?"

"Just a little," he said looking at the floor. "I was trying to hear what you were saying. I only did a little spell."

I pulled him into the bathroom and made him look in the mirror. "See?"

His face broke into a huge grin. "That's pretty. How did it happen?"

I would be glad to have Lionel back. At least he was consistent. Inlackt sometimes seemed as adult as me or Trahaearn, and other times he was like a child. "The prophecy."

"That's not good," he said, suddenly back to the adult version.

I shook my head and gave him a push toward the door. "No. Now let's eat before we make any more mistakes. Beacon will be back in a minute."

He followed me to the kitchen where the table was laid and covered with food. I should have been too worried to eat, but something about the meal radiated comfort and confidence. I looked at Trahaearn and noticed the faint amber glow. "You won't be able to go out either. I guess most of us will be stuck in place for a while."

"We needed courage, and the spell was small." He carved the chicken and served. "Anyway, we need some gauge of how long the glow lasts. If we can define a timeline, it will help those of us who can choose not to do magic. Beacon will protect the park, but we need to talk to the others. The sidhe, the trolls, pixies, and whatever else lives in this town."

"What about other towns?" I asked. "Your grove?"

"They will have noticed. I'll contact them through the circle later. They will manage the area." He sounded calm, but I could see the way his tattoos moved. His body carried a lot of tension.

"We'll figure out how to warn everyone before we go back to the amulet." The danger was greater to us, who live in this world, than it was to Lionel. At least, for a little while.

21

Beacon returned as we finished the last of the meal. Dionne cleared the table and made Inlackt help her with the dishes. She was trying to distract him from doing any more magic. He'd been casting tiny spells throughout the meal. I heard her tell him that he couldn't clean the dishes with magic, and I despaired of Lionel ever getting out of the house with the glow he would inherit. We'd starve to death because we wouldn't be able to go to the store.

Beacon accepted a beer and gave us an update. "Everyone will be in the deepest part of the park before moon rise. The fairies have called all the outlying tribes to hide and only travel in the light. There will be no fairies, imps, or sprites outside the park by tomorrow night."

Part of me was relieved, but a big part was sad. Having no fairies, imps, or sprites, the other parks would be less fertile, less welcoming. "We'll find a way to make it safe again."

Beacon nodded. "I hope so. Having us so concentrated isn't good for the park either."

"We need to get a warning out," I said. "Before we deal with Inlackt and Lionel, we need to give everyone a chance to survive."

"Let's get started," Trahaearn said. "We can do this without Dionne and Inlackt. They are still glowing. We need them to be magic free for a while longer. Beacon, we will need you as a witness, and perhaps protection."

We were still glowing, but I saw his point. Someone had to do magic to warn everyone. Those two could be the control group. "Dionne," I called. "You and Inlackt need to stay magic free."

"Yes, Quinn, I promise I'll be good," Dionne said with a stern look to Inlackt.

"Why do I have to be good?" Inlackt asked. "I'll be in the amulet. No one will care if I glow."

Beacon placed his hand on my arm as I started to respond. He shook his head at me. "No, Quinn, the sprite will answer to my authority. Inlackt, that body does not belong to you. Do not make it glow any more than it already is."

"Yes, Beacon," he answered cheerfully. Apparently, Beacon wasn't someone to sulk at.

When the three of us were settled within a salt circle, Trahaearn asked, "Do you have any ideas?"

I nodded. "The only local Real Folk left are the sidhe and anyone at Banks'. I can contact the court. They can send someone through the tunnel to warn everyone to stay at Banks' or the court, until daylight and not do magic. Maeve will have to pull her guards in and lock the doors."

I called Melbe to the circle, trying not to let the brewing panic come through in my summons. His head formed in a ghostly shimmer. "What do you want, wizard? We are busy."

I explained why I had called. "Can you get someone through to Banks'?"

"Wait," he said, his attitude unchanging despite the knowledge. A few seconds later he returned. "Maeve will send warning. She thanks you for the explanation. She also requires you to find a solution since you are the one who brought the prophecy about."

It felt like I would never reduce my list of problems to solve.

"We're on it," I said. "We have to go. More people need our warning."

Melbe's head disappeared back into the dirt of the floor.

Next, we called Haruto, Herminia, Dai, and Tamrat. Each popped into the circle as if they had been waiting for the call. "Yes, we know," Herminia said for all four. "We have given warning to those we can reach."

"Good," I said. "We'll find a way to send some general warning to the world.

"Use your spirits," Haruto said. "That one, Ranseed, will do as you ask. He relies on the power of Real Folk for his existence."

That was interesting. I would be factoring that into negotiations in future. "Thank you. I would prefer that be our secret."

"Indeed," Haruto chuckled. "Knowledge is real power in this situation. Now we must go. This is too much magic to hide even in the full glow of the sun.

All four dust images collapsed.

I wanted to keep going, but fairness made me stop and ask, "Trahaearn, do you want to contact your grove?"

He looked up from the ground where he'd been focused. He wasn't using the power, I would have felt it, but he was definitely concentrating on something. My hope was that he'd come up with a solution, but my reality was that he'd probably found another problem. There was gratitude in his eyes, so maybe he was only worried. "Yes, then we will use your spirit to warn the world." He slipped out of his shoes and placed his skin on the soil.

The power warmed, and I heard Beacon grunt. "That is similar to my power."

Trahaearn looked up from the soil. "Yes, it's earth magic. A different variety to yours, not so nurturing. I cannot heal growing things as effortlessly as you, but I use the pathways of the earth to access my power."

We waited while he seemed to only stare at the dirt. Then he looked up and reached for his shoes. "They are safe. The Real

Folk took refuge in the grove, and are searching the records for any solution. There are far fewer of us there. To be honest, it is a wonder how many Real Folk live in Vancouver."

Time to call Ranseed. I threw three candies to the dirt and held four more in reserve. "Ranseed, come to the circle."

The rush of wind and rustle of leaves followed immediately on my words. "Quinn Larson, there is much excitement in the world."

"Yes, what will it cost for you to send a message to all Real Folk?"

"What message?"

Surprised at his lack of foreplay, I considered. I was going to pay whatever he asked, but Haruto's news was still in my mind. "This message will save the Real Folk, and anyone who relies on them."

"Ten candies. I will not ask a favor."

Why did it have to be difficult? "I only have eight candies. I do not have time to get more."

He chuckled. "Yes, urgent. I will allow you to owe me two candies."

"Deal." I threw the others on the dirt.

He spun them into the center of the circle. "Very well, what is this message?"

I shut down the little voice that said it was too easy. "The prophecy has brought a dangerous change to the world. Magic makes Real Folk glow. It means humans can identify them. Humans will know about us, and that usually means someone dies."

The sound of wind through dead leaves filled our ears. "Yes. And that would cause others to no longer exist."

"How long before the world will know?" Trahaearn asked.

"Minutes, druid. How long before you have a solution?"

I didn't like this casual chat. I was accustomed to tightly controlling the communication with the spirit. I held up a hand for silence. "Ranseed, do not overreach. We will find a solution. But for now, those who are magic, must hide and those who do magic must refrain."

The leaves rattled again, this time I thought I felt a touch of fear in the sound. Was that Ranseed's fear, or was he trying to instill fear in us? It didn't matter now; time had run out. As the sound died, he asked, "And if they have already done magic?"

He was fishing for information and normally I would deny him the details, but this was too important. "The glow will fade over time, but we do not know how long it will take, or if using magic repeatedly will affect that."

"Call me when you have more information." He left and the candies sank into the ground.

"We've done what we can," I said clearing the circle.

Beacon stayed on the ground. "We should send Inlackt back now."

Trahaearn stood. "I'll bring them. Quinn. We need to postpone freeing my druids. I do not think it safe for us to do such magic here. We will need to go to the grove before doing magic."

I watched him go. He came here to stop the pain he was feeling. Everything since he arrived had conspired to get between him and that goal. He hadn't mentioned the pain recently, but it must still be there, and would likely stay until the druids were released.

Trahaearn returned with Dionne and Inlackt. To my great relief, Dionne no longer glowed. Inlackt still had a faint shimmer of cobalt to him, but it was much fainter than before. It was information at least. We'd need more tests, but perhaps the glow was manageable for wizards.

I closed a circle around us and lowered myself onto the ground. "Dionne, sit next to me. Beacon, can you sit behind Inlackt and keep contact?" He shifted to make room and told Inlackt to sit before him. "Trahaearn, will you lead us through?" It did feel good to be in charge, however fleeting and ineffective it was.

Inlackt tried to move away from Beacon. "That is a bad place for me. I don't want to go back. This world is better even with the curse."

I couldn't deny his fears, the amulet scared me. I tried reason. "It is not a curse. It is just a change. We will find a way to live with it. Now, you agreed to go back."

"I've changed my mind." He struggled, but Beacon held him down.

"Inlackt," Beacon said. "You need to do as you agreed. But I will not leave you there. I promise."

It wasn't like Beacon to lie so he must have a plan. Maybe hearing it would settle Inlackt long enough to make the exchange. "What are you saying Beacon?"

He dug into his pocket. "I brought this." He held up a lump of mud. "When Lionel is back in his body, I will come for you, Inlackt. Then you can live in the plant that grows from the seed in this earth."

Inlackt squinted at the green lump in Beacon's hand. "What kind of plant?" He didn't sound suspicious, more like he wanted to make sure he would like the plant.

Beacon smiled. "An oak."

Inlackt beamed. Trees must have some kind of status value to the sprites. Clearly an oak was a good home.

Inlackt squirmed in Beacon's grasp. "Can I go there now? Why do I have to go back to the amulet?"

Trahaearn reached for Inlackt and Dionne's hands. When the contact was complete between all of us, he said, "Because we cannot guarantee Lionel will be able to return to a body that you have deserted. Now, let's get this done."

Inlackt still looked worried.

"I promise," I said, "we will not leave you in that world. We will work to free you as soon as Lionel has his body back."

He looked at me with an intensity that could have bored

through my skull and penetrated my mind. "I will trust you, Quinn Larson. I have no choice."

That wasn't good enough. For all I knew, he could maroon us in the amulet and fill our bodies with his friends. Of course, trust breeds trust, I suppose. "Inlackt, you always have a choice. We will not force you from Lionel's body. If you don't trust Beacon's word, or mine, who will you trust?"

He slumped. "I trust you. I don't want to go back there. You brought Lionel back to his body before when it was empty."

I looked at Trahaearn for assistance, but he was focused on the dirt under us. Dionne saved me from trying to answer.

"Inlackt," she said gently. "When we did that, Lionel's body was preserved. If you leave it, how do we know that it will stay alive long enough to get him back?"

"You could preserve it again."

I tried not to hear slyness in his tone. We had changed the world together. We should be able to get a sprite to go back to the amulet for a few minutes. "Beacon, can you take the seed with us into the amulet? That way Inlackt can move from Lionel's body directly to his new home."

Inlackt brightened and twisted to look at Beacon who said, "I don't think so. From what you have said, this amulet is not a place to take anything but your spirit."

Trahaearn returned from whatever meditation he'd been lost in. "Have Inlackt hold the seed. That way he can make the switch as Lionel takes over the body."

I looked at the sprite. "Will that be enough?"

He took the mud ball from Beacon. Holding it carefully in his fingertips, he turned and rolled it before his eyes. "Yes. I won't go to the amulet. When you have Lionel, I will move to my new body, and he can flow into this one."

That was an angle I would never have considered. "Beacon will you be able to signal Inlackt?"

"Do you have control of your body when you are in there?"

Thinking back to Trahaearn's reactions, and Dionne's running away I couldn't be sure. "Possibly. Dionne, when you left us to look for Lionel, how did you manage not to break the contact we had here?"

She reached for my hand. "I just told my body not to move. Then I went."

"Okay, Inlackt. Beacon will do something to let you know we have Lionel."

"Good, now go and get him so I can begin my new life."

Trahaearn made us join hands. Beacon and I each took one of Inlackt's.

"Close your eyes and focus on my voice," Trahaearn said. "You will see my spirit flow with the words. Follow my spirit to the amulet."

I saw a trail of amber motes forming his words in my mind. Then it arrowed off toward a pinpoint of rose light. We burst through the entrance to the amulet and stood together. Lionel was not there. I wasn't surprised. It is not like a bus stop where he could sit and wait. And Lionel's curiosity would have drawn him further in to gather any tendrils of knowledge that might exist here.

It wasn't as frightening this time. The blazing lights and hurricane winds were gone. The place felt deserted. It wasn't any comfort to be here when it was abandoned, but at least I could think.

"Dionne, please call for Lionel," Trahaearn said. He was looking around, his face drawn.

Dionne called, but Lionel didn't come.

"Can you feel him?" I asked.

"Faintly," she said. "Should I go looking?" She was practically vibrating with the need to go searching.

I said she should wait. I didn't want to lose her in whatever had taken the other souls. "Trahaearn, do you sense the druids?"

"They are here. I am not happy that it is so quiet. Not that the madness before was good. I fear that the prophecy has affected this world. That my druids will not return."

If the souls of the druids were gone, we would be killing the vampires for no reason. "If you can feel them, we must still have time. If we can't return them, what will happen?"

Before he could answer Dionne announced, "Lionel is coming. Look." She pointed to her right. I couldn't see anything, and I had to tell my nerves that she was still holding my hand in the real world. If I concentrated, I could feel the light touch of her fingers.

Gradually a glow approached. "Is it done?" Lionel asked as he coalesced from a ball of white motes into a facsimile of his real body.

"Yes," I answered, amazed at how he had changed. He was almost comfortable in this world. "What happened here?"

He looked around. "I managed to make a connection with a few of the souls. They know what is happening. The more sane ones have gone to gather the others, so that when you release them they will be ready."

"Are you sure there are no other repercussions?" Trahaearn asked. "The prophecy has not affected this world."

"It looks like we're okay," I said. I was anxious to get out of here with my apprentice back in his body.

"It is important. My druids need to remain here until we can manage to get to the grove and overcome the vampires." Trahaearn kept looking around as though expecting to see a host of druids approaching.

"There have been no changes," Lionel insisted. "If you are worried, I can stay until you bring all of the souls out."

"No." I was not going to risk Lionel. "We had a deal. If Lionel says there has been no change, then we need to go. The sooner we complete this exchange, the sooner we can stop doing magic long enough to be able to walk to the grove."

Trahaearn seemed about to argue and then thought better of

it. "Fine. We have a task to perform then. Beacon, please let Inlackt know it is time."

Beacon frowned. "He is still concerned. I see I will have an unruly oak in my care for a while." His lips moved, and then he nodded. "Okay, Lionel, as you go in, he will leave."

"Let him know that it is quiet here, so he won't be too afraid of the change," Lionel said.

I told him what we were doing with the sprite and he nodded. "It would be wonderful if we could store the other souls outside this amulet. But I guess, it will not be long now before they are safe."

We watched as Lionel's form exploded into the ball of motes again. This time the ball compressed upon itself until the last of the lights blinked out. Trahaearn led us back to the real world as soon as that happened.

I opened my eyes to see Lionel looking around the circle. He held the mud ball in his hand, and we all glowed with enough energy to read an ancient, faded, spell book by.

❧ 22 ☙

It was clear when we returned to the kitchen that we weren't going anywhere until the sun could cover our glows. I pulled beers and soda from the fridge.

"Aw, Quinn. I live here now. Can't I have a beer?" Dionne pouted.

"No. We have too much to do to find out how you react to alcohol." I handed her the soda. "Anyway, you may not like it."

She opened the soda and took a long drink, covering her mouth when the inevitable belch exploded. We all laughed.

Trahaearn reached for the bottle opener. "I have to admit this prophecy is going to make things much less convenient until we find a way to exist with the humans. Or to disguise our nature, I suppose."

Lionel sat quietly on one of the stools. I was surprised he didn't ask what the prophecy had changed. "I think we start by bringing Lionel up to date."

An hour later, Lionel stopped us. "I think that's enough detail for now. Since I don't hear rioting outside, I assume the humans haven't figured it out yet."

I looked out the window. It was pouring with rain. "I think

they're inside. We have some time." I could only hope for weeks of this downpour. "No magic until we get to the museum."

"I should do something so Beacon can go back to the park," Dionne said. "I can do that charm spell. That way, I'll be faded before we go out, and Beacon doesn't have to do magic to hide." She ran to the workroom as soon as I gave permission.

The young were so adaptable, it made me envious. "Do that then no more, Dionne. I guess we'll be sleeping on the floor tonight. We'll find a way to get you a room. Trahaearn, will you want to stay here after we heal your druids?"

He glanced at the couch and then shook his head. "Thank you for the invitation, but I will be at the museum."

I realized the social niceties were just a delaying tactic. We were going to need to make our plans. "Let's work out the details then."

Dionne returned from the workroom with a pinecone in one hand and a snail shell in the other. She handed Beacon the pinecone. "Just give it a squeeze a few minutes before we leave and you'll be fine."

"Trahaearn," I said returning to the planning discussion. "What do you think we will need to take with us?"

"I need only to have some contact with growing things. You may want to fill your pockets with charms. I don't think we will be able to avoid casting spells, so you may want to plan to stay with us in the grove for as long as it takes your glows to fade."

"Okay. Lionel, you and Dionne need to make sure no one comes to the door while we're gone. I don't think Ms. Metcalfe is quite done with us yet."

"What do you mean?" Dionne said. "We'll be with you."

"No, just Trahaearn and I will go. I will not change my mind."

Out of the corner of my eye, I saw Beacon and Trahaearn share a glance. They stood and went to the living room. It wasn't far enough away for privacy, but at least they wouldn't get drawn in. I didn't like the fact that the glance they'd shared seemed to involve a smirk.

"Quinn, you will need both of us there. If there are four of us, we will each do less magic," Lionel said. "And I have a grievance to settle with them. If they had been honest, you would have known how to release me from the amulet earlier."

The only argument I could think of was to appeal to his protective instinct. I knew that if I allowed Lionel to join us, Dionne would not remain in the house. "Dionne can't be seen. If someone recognizes her, she could be sent back to her foster parents. What happens if she starts to glow because she does some magic."

"Oh, I can take care of that," she said. "I made this charm at the same time." She held up the snail shell. "I just crush it, and I look like I'm younger, and a boy."

"They are not going to just lie down and let us trade their spirits," I said. "It will be dangerous. I don't want you to get hurt."

"Life is dangerous for us now, Quinn," Dionne said. "You need to let us help."

In my mind, I could hear my master tell me that I should just obey his orders because I was the apprentice. I hated it then, and didn't want to repeat the experience for my apprentices. It never worked on me anyway, and I was pretty obedient. These two were about as compliant as the wind and the sun. Recognizing I was fighting a lost battle, I started setting boundaries. "You will heed me and Trahaearn. If we say run, you run. If we say hide, you disappear. I will not lose either of you to this fight."

Dionne jumped up and hugged me. "I knew you'd see the sense of it."

I unwrapped her arms and looked into her eyes. "Dionne, I am not kidding around. I have a very strong feeling that you will be part of finding a way for the Real Folk to survive. This isn't a game. If the humans... no, when the humans realize we exist, there will be blood. On both sides of the fight."

She lost her smile and the joy that had fueled it. "I know, Quinn. Remember, my parents were killed because of the prophecy. I think it's possible that the vampires did it so the prophecy wouldn't happen."

I jerked away. "What makes you think that?"

"They have done everything they can to stop it. It's like they knew exactly what would happen. So, killing my parents isn't a leap, right?"

It was possible, even probable, but we would likely never know. "They must have known that something like this would happen. The last time humans found Real Folk, it was the vampires. They were slaughtered. The humans would drag them out into the light and watch as they burst into flames."

"I've never heard of this," she said. "When did it happen?"

"Not that long ago in terms of our lifetimes, but humans have a tendency to bury information they think might be dangerous. It would not be hard to confuse the history into folklore."

Trahaearn joined us at the counter. I looked over and saw that Beacon was lying on the floor – the entire floor – of my living room. "I hope we can all rest as easily tonight," I said.

There was a crease of worry on his brow. "Quinn, we need to plan. I promise that I will ensure Dionne is trained in any history you wish, but we need to retake the museum if that promise is to mean anything."

I motioned for him to start.

"As you said, they will not just lie down and let us remove their souls. But that gave me an idea." He leaned in conspiratorially. "The best plan is a simple one. I say we spell them to sleep. When they are under, we replace the druid souls. The vampires can occupy the amulet until we find a better punishment."

I hadn't expected the plan to be that simple. "Shouldn't we have some contingencies? I know that once we fight, all plans go out the door, but that just seems too easy."

"If they resist, we will fight. We cannot kill the bodies, or the druids will have no home."

Lionel pushed away from the counter. "I do not feel the need to rest. Dionne can take my bed. I will research as many immobilization spells as I can find. We can study them over breakfast."

Going into battle with spells we hadn't practiced was foolish. Delaying so we could practice was probably suicide. "Wake us early enough that we can prepare."

We separated to find our rest. Trahaearn asked my permission to sleep on my dirt floor. "If you need to take some of the power, feel free," I said. "We probably won't be doing any circle work until we've figured this problem out."

23

The museum was quiet when we arrived. It showed no evidence of being a den of body stealing vampires. The trees surrounding it were old, and now I was aware it was supposed to be a grove, I noticed that they formed a perfect circle. The low shrubs and undergrowth did a good job of disguising the symmetry of the trees. The museum itself was a stone building like a small, round, Gothic style church.

Trahaearn asked us to stay near the door while he walked the perimeter. I watched as he placed his hand on each trunk and stopped for a moment before passing onto the next. Each visit causing him to glow a little brighter. As he passed, the trees seemed to become more of a presence. The tiny sounds that filled the city, not just the birds and scurrying animals, but the sound of traffic and people, dampened. It felt like we were in a room rather than a small urban forest.

Then he was around the back of the building, and I found myself wondering why no one had come out to see what we wanted. Surely Myrddin was aware we were outside.

"They are waiting for us," Lionel said, answering my unspoken question. "I can feel them."

He hadn't been able to sense people from a distance before. I wondered if it was because of the amulet, or if we were seeing more effects of the prophecy. "What do you mean?"

"The time I was in the amulet, when I was talking to the druids, letting them know that we would free them, they told me how to unlock the magic of the museum. I can sense what's going on, because I've sent some of my power inside. My power is all I've managed to get in. I don't think I can get us past the locking spells."

Did none of my apprentices feel the need to obey? "I thought you were going to let us do all the work," I said.

"We are," Dionne said. "Lionel isn't doing any work. He's reconnoitering the situation."

"Don't get caught," I said. If I couldn't control them, I would try to keep them safe.

Trahaearn came into view and did whatever he was doing to the last three trees before joining us. "The trees will keep humans out. It's what they do in a healthy grove. Or at least, part of what they do."

"How come they don't glow?" Dionne moved to the closest tree. "Oh, they aren't doing magic, or holding magic like the charm."

"They will if a human comes near enough to trigger the avoidance spell. Otherwise, they are just trees," he said. "More or less."

I told him what Lionel had learned. "Can you get us inside?"

"I can," Trahaearn said. "I have a master spell for all groves. Perhaps it won't be necessary, look."

The door to the museum was opening. Myrddin stepped out and stood with his back against it. As we walked toward him, he held up a hand to stop us, then leaned on the door to close it. "Wait, do not come closer."

We had agreed to pretend we didn't know what was going on until we were able to get inside and contain the fight. Facing a group of desperate vampires in the open was guaranteed to be harder than fighting inside a building.

Trahaearn stepped in front of our small group. "I am your arch druid; you must allow me to enter."

Myrddin blinked. He was not expecting to be taken for a druid. "We are not prepared for visitors. We are trying to find a cure for this glowing plague."

Trahaearn stepped closer and beckoned us to follow. We had Myrddin backed tight against the door. His eyes widened. "Please, do not harm us."

"We know who you are," I said. "Myrddin, let us inside, or we will force our way in." I hoped he'd obey. I wanted to conserve our power for the actual battle.

"No, please let me explain. You must understand what happened." He was trembling. It was pathetic. I couldn't tell if he was acting to get us off our guard, or if he was truly terrified.

"Quinn, don't listen to him." Trahaearn's voice was harsh and I could feel anger from him, hot and powerful.

"We would have died," Myrddin said. "We didn't know it would be so long. We thought we could share the bodies until we could find other vessels."

Trahaearn pressed his hand on the door. It started to open outward, pushing Myrddin toward us. "Get out of my way," he said. "You stole the bodies of the druids. You couldn't have done that by accident. You sent them to a place of madness, and lied about them."

Myrddin pushed back against the door. I don't know what he was trying to do, but it was clear he needed to delay us. "Lionel, can you tell what is happening inside?"

He closed his eyes to concentrate. "I can only tell that someone is doing magic. It is powerful."

Dionne squeezed past me. "Myrddin, whatever you are planning, give it up. If you fight us, it will go badly for you. If you let us in, we can find a place for your souls. It doesn't have to mean your death." Her hand touched him, and he screamed.

"Dionne, step back," Trahaearn shouted. "Do not allow him any access to you. We do not know how they took the bodies."

She took her hand off Myrddin. "He can't do anything to me."

I pushed her behind me. "Why is he screaming?"

She rolled her eyes. "I don't know. I just thought if we knew his secrets, we could get through the door faster. Something is going on in there, and I'm worried it's something that will attack us."

Myrddin stopped screaming and tried to run. Trahaearn caught him by the hood of his jacket. "No, we will need that body for the original owner. But you will be quiet." Myrddin's voice stopped. His lips moved, but no sound emerged. Trahaearn pulled the door open far enough for us to slip inside, dragging Myrddin with us.

The hall was full of trash, but empty of people. Lionel's description of the museum conflicted so strongly with the actuality that I almost stopped to test if we were looking at an illusion. I could feel power building in one of the rooms. Lionel must have been presented with an illusion before. That was the only explanation that made sense. "What can we do to neutralize him?" Lionel asked. "Or were you planning to drag him with us the whole time?"

Trahaearn looked into Myrddin's eyes, then I saw his tattoo glow. "I think we'll drag him along. If we keep them together, it will be easier to control them." He removed his belt and used it to tie Myrddin's hands. "Dionne, what did you learn?"

"They invaded the druids," she whispered. "The druids were trying to protect them from the humans. They were trying to save the vampires. It left them vulnerable. The vampires just invaded. The druids were using the amulet as a focusing device. That's how they ended up inside."

Myrddin tried to escape. Trahaearn jerked on the belt, and

Myrddin landed on his back. "Do not fight me. I will damage that body if you make me. I can have it healed later."

"Quinn, we need to act. That power is building," Lionel said.

Myrddin did his best to slow us down, but between Trahaearn yanking on the belt and Dionne shoving, we made progress toward the room where I could feel power being used. "Get some defensive spells ready," I told Dionne and Lionel.

They pulled charms from their pockets and started breaking the containers. We left a trail of peanut shells, and dust from dried mud, in our wake. The glow of magic formed around us. I motioned for them to fall back as we approached the archway to the room.

"Tell them to stop whatever they are doing," Trahaearn ordered Myrddin. "Save your brothers."

Myrddin shook his head so violently that his entire body rocked.

Trahaearn turned to Dionne. "Can you heal the wounds that the bodies will receive?"

She handed Lionel the charms she hadn't yet activated. "As long as I have power, I can heal some pretty bad stuff. If they die, I can't bring them back."

How did she know that? The only training I'd done with her was basic. We knew she could heal, but there was nothing to support her confidence. I didn't say anything, because sometimes confidence was more important than training.

Trahaearn made to step into the room and the lights blew. We could still see. Real Folk are able to see in the dark, but also, we were glowing, and so was the room. The glows left shadows that shifted when we moved.

"Take this one," Trahaearn said handing Lionel the belt. "Stay out here until you are needed."

"How will we know," Dionne asked. So, she was able to just do as she was told. I might have to get some tips from Trahaearn when we were done.

He smiled at her. "Either we will call you, or you will know we need help." He stepped through the archway. I was one pace behind him.

Power balls flew at us from all sides. There were twenty druids in the room, scattered around. It would be difficult for us to retaliate with them so spread out.

Trahaearn threw a spell out to stop the balls. They bounced off some kind of shield, but didn't go back to the druids who'd cast them. They dropped to the ground and dissipated.

He stared at the druids as he said, "Just as we agreed, Quinn. Attack to disable."

"Leave us in peace," someone called from a far corner of the room.

I realized we were in lab of some kind. There were tables with jars filled with mysterious lumps, and bowls filled with powders. I saw some animal parts and what looked like a human hand on a bench.

"Like you left the druids?" Trahaearn shouted as he threw a spell that unfurled into a golden net. He followed it with a second net, and then a third.

The nets caught four of the druids and tangled them into a heap. As they struggled to free themselves, I tossed sleep charms at them. I made contact, and the false druids fell asleep. "It will last about an hour," I reminded Trahaearn.

"We need to do something stronger," he said. "We cannot stop them a few at a time."

"If they keep scattered, we won't have a choice. Is this all of them?"

"I sense no others, and this is a normal grove size. Thirteen full druids and about half that number of students."

He threw two more nets, but the druids dodged. Fortunately, their movements brought them together. "Trahaearn, did you see that?"

"Yes, keep herding them." He was busy getting his nets ready.

I tossed some charms to the side of the largest group of druids. The charms exploded. They were harmless, but loud and bright. The druids moved together again. We had two loose groups of them. Trahaearn tossed a net and captured six of them in one swoop. I followed it with more sleep charms. It was going to be easier than I had feared. The vampires were not good at battle strategy. They had started out well enough, but they couldn't stop crowding together.

Trahaearn moved to cast another net. I saw that he was making it large enough to cover the remaining druids. I only had four sleep charms, but I knew a spell I could cast without ingredients. Not my favorite way to enter a fight, but still possible, although it would weaken me.

"Ready?" Trahaearn asked, pulling his arm back to cast.

"I will be," I answered as I looked in my pocket for the final charm.

I heard a grunt beside me and looked up. Trahaearn was collapsing, a stream of blood running from his arm. I shot a glance at the group of druids, four of them were struggling against the net. The other six were retreating to opposite sides of the room. I tossed the final sleep charms I held, and most of the struggling stopped. The two druids who weren't sleeping were trapped under their comrades.

"Dionne," I called as I bent to pull Trahaearn clear. He was limp and heavy. I dragged him to the archway where Dionne was running toward us.

"Stay outside," I said. "We'll seal them in here."

She helped me drag Trahaearn through to the hall. As soon as we were out of the room, she shouted, "Lionel, cast the web."

A rush of air passed my head and I looked up to see a web of light covering the opening.

"It will hold them there for long enough for us to fix this," Lionel said. He helped me pull Trahaearn's arm away from where it was curled against his side. The arch druid was unconscious.

His skin paler than normal. The glow of his magic was pulsing through the blood that soaked his shirt. With each pulse, the glow returned duller.

"What happened?" Lionel asked.

"I wasn't watching him. Someone must have thrown a knife or something. His arm was up to cast a spell. They were cowering. I thought we had won, and it was just a matter of cleaning up." Panic started to shatter my thoughts. If he didn't recover, we wouldn't be able to get back into the amulet to free the souls.

I refused to succumb to the irrational fear. "Dionne, could you cast the spells you used on Lionel? If we can preserve the bodies, maybe we can find another druid to perform the spell to rejoin them."

Lionel glanced at the web spell he'd cast. "I don't know, Quinn. It might be a problem. It was my soul she separated from my body. What if it won't work if the soul isn't the right one?"

Dionne pushed Lionel to the side. "Will you stop worrying about what we're going to do next? We need to save Trahaearn." She pulled a small plastic bottle from her pocket and squirted a blob of clear liquid into her palm.

"What's that?" Lionel asked.

"Hand sanitizer." She rubbed her hands together. "I don't want to make it worse."

24

"He's alive," Dionne said. "Quinn let me get at that arm. We have to stop the bleeding first."

She pushed me out of the way and pressed both of her hands against the gaping wound. Her glow merged with his. She muttered a few words, and when she removed her hands, the wound was closed. "Dionne, how did you learn that?" I asked.

"When we did the rite for the prophecy, Haruto and Herminia gave us each some knowledge. I got healing." She said it in such a matter of fact tone that I wondered if she was hiding some other knowledge she'd gained.

Her glow was dimming, but I didn't think it was because of her magic, more likely her life energy. "Lionel, can you check to see if he is okay?" she asked weakly.

Lionel bent and checked Trahaearn's pulse before placing his hand on the druid's forehead. After a few minutes, he said, "He's weak, but he's getting better."

We needed him to be more than just getting better. "Is there some exposed earth around?" It would make sense they would have some, if druids got their strength that way.

"There might be under all this mess," Dionne said. "But we

don't have time to dig it up." She knelt and placed her hands on Trahaearn's exposed tattoos.

I reached to stop her, but it was too late. "Dionne, don't drain yourself." The words came out even though I knew she'd already crossed the line by the pallor of her skin and the way she slumped. The glow of energy between them was now gone. Dionne had barely a glimmer, but Trahaearn shone.

"You should have stopped her, Quinn," Trahaearn said as he pushed himself off the floor. "We will need her healing skills for the druids."

I reached for his hand and pulled him the rest of the way to his feet. "You think I didn't try?" I tilted my head toward the room behind us. "I need you too. That web won't last long, and we're getting to the edge of the sleep spell. Can we argue later? I don't want to have to start this battle from the beginning again."

Lionel cradled Dionne in his arms. "I'll restore her. We'll have time to share power while you fight."

It wasn't the best solution. We would have two apprentices with only half their power, if that. But this was battle, and nothing was ever perfect in a fight. "Okay, keep your eyes on Myrddin, and wait for us to call."

"Quinn, be careful," Dionne said.

I smiled at her. The glow of light between Lionel's hands was already building her strength. "I will be as careful as I can. Do you still have charms?"

They both dug into their pockets. "I have these," Lionel said holding out a handful of hazelnuts. "Mostly distraction, flashes, and noises, nothing lethal."

"I have a few repel charms," Dionne said. "If we had more power, we could create more." She pointed to the debris that had blown into the hall over the years. Nuts, leaves, and fronds were scattered around. "As soon as we can, we'll make some nets, or stun spells."

"Don't tax yourself," Trahaearn said. "Can you take power from the earth?"

"I can," Lionel said. "I can teach Dionne. But where is there enough earth to hold power?"

Trahaearn glared at Myrddin who was still struggling against his bonds. "If this place had been cared for, you wouldn't have to ask." He kicked at a pile of books that had fallen from the shelves. "If you move this, you should find earth. If not, you may have to go out to the grove."

"No," I said. "No one leaves until we are done. I don't trust that there are no traps to lock the doors behind anyone who goes outside."

Trahaearn pulled my arm. "The web is being attacked. We need to finish this."

I didn't want to leave my two apprentices in their weakened state. If I worried about them while we were fighting, it could mean disaster. I looked to the web covering the archway. It was fraying. The glow of power disintegrating into motes at the edges.

"When we break through, take the remaining power back. When you have the first stun charm, use it on Myrddin." I turned away to race after Trahaearn.

We touched the web on opposite sides. It pulled away from the stone. I whipped it over my head toward Lionel and Dionne before stepping into the room.

The situation hadn't changed much. The four druids we'd left free had managed to untangle the nets, but the sleep spells held. The two who had been trapped under their fallen brothers were still on the floor. I noticed an arm laying awkwardly, probably broken, and the other was holding his head as though afraid it would fall off.

"Don't discount the injured ones," Trahaearn said. "They may still be able to cast spells, or sharp objects." He rubbed his wound.

The four mobile druids were scattered around the room.

Apparently, they had finally learned some battle skill. "Any ideas?" I didn't think this impasse would last long.

"Can you stun them?" Trahaearn asked as he reached for a long pipe that had fallen from the apparatus on the closest bench.

I liked his ingenuity, but I thought we were trying to preserve the bodies. "How are you going to use that without doing serious damage?"

He grinned at me. "Dionne can heal a broken limb. When we're done here, she will have time to restore her energy before we need to rescue the souls. The vampires will feel the pain, not the druids."

I didn't like the glint in his eyes, but I had to trust that he had the restraint he needed. "Cover me while I gather ingredients."

"Do it fast," he said. "They aren't waiting for us to be ready."

I watched him cast a spell of protection around us. A dome of rainbow light that formed just as a heavy jar flew toward us. One for protection, one for attack, I thought. The smallest fighting unit outside of a duel. And right now, Trahaearn was covering both roles.

I looked at what was to hand. Trahaearn had included a case full of bottles and jars in the protective spell. I found rosemary and pepper on one shelf. They were old but still usable. I rubbed them between my fingers and chanted the words that would turn the powder in to a mist I could direct. "Ready? Let the barrier down."

Trahaearn used the pipe to bat away a rock that flew at us as the dome collapsed. I ignored the distraction and chanted again. The mist formed an arrow and shot from my palms. I aimed it at the two injured druids, catching a third who rushed to aid them, all three collapsed into a heap. There were only three druids left conscious, but they were spread out so far that we couldn't take them down as a group.

"I think we have about fifteen minutes left on the original

spell," I said. I couldn't be more accurate, time passed weirdly in battle, but I could feel the spell weaken as I spoke.

"We'll have to get in close," Trahaearn said. "Do you have enough of that spell left to take out the one in the far corner?" He was careful not to point at the intended target.

I glanced at where the vampire stood, half cowering, half defiant. I was suddenly very grateful for the prophecy. A day ago, he would have been hidden in shadows, but now he glowed an acid green. There was no hiding from the attack. "I can make more, but it's a one-shot deal."

He hefted his pipe. "Can you protect yourself enough to advance?"

I felt in my pockets before answering. There were occasionally charms in the bottom that I'd forgotten. This time I came up empty.

"I cannot protect you and still attack separately," Trahaearn said. "They are preparing something."

"I'll just have to dodge anything they send." I scanned the area between me and the cornered druid.

"Duck, Quinn," Dionne's voice called before I saw a hazel nut arc over us.

I pulled Trahaearn to the ground just before the flash exploded.

As soon as the spell activated, I yanked him from the floor and shoved him in the direction of the farthest druid. "We'll meet in the center."

I rushed the corner. The split-second warning had allowed us to avoid the worst of the glare, leaving my sight faded, but still usable. I hoped the same was true of Trahaearn.

As I ran, I picked up a few things that I needed. There was no time to gather a spell, but there was plenty of time to gather an old rag and a rope that were lying handy. I would never complain about messes again. Now when I saw a pile of discarded items, I would see treasure.

It took only seconds to reach my target, but he was already shaking off the effects of the flash. I barreled into him, knocking the wind out of both of us. I ignored the pain and rolled him onto his back, tying his hands as he tried to buck me off. I looped the rope through an iron pipe that was bolted to the wall. I shoved the rag into his mouth to silence him and levered myself off.

I looked to where the other druid stood, the one Trahaearn attacked. There were sparks of magic flashing between them. Dionne's charm hadn't been as effective for that one, and it was good that Trahaearn was a better warrior than I was.

Movement caught my attention, and I saw the third druid heading for the doorway. There was no chance that Dionne and Lionel had recovered enough to defend themselves. I trusted Trahaearn to hold his own and ran to catch the escaping one.

"Stop," I yelled. He paid no attention. The only thing slowing him down was the debris. If I moved fast enough, maybe I could grab his robe and pull him down.

I ran, feeling my feet slipping on items scattered across the floor, not caring if I hurt myself, knowing I would keep going through any pain to save Dionne and Lionel.

My headlong rush brought me within arm's reach of the fleeing druid. I could hear him mumbling, getting a spell ready to cast. I couldn't tell what it was, I just knew it wouldn't be anything pleasant.

I leapt toward him and grabbed at the back of his robe. It had a greasy consistency, like it hadn't been washed in years. It started to slip from my fingers, and I yanked. The druid jerked off his feet and fell to the floor. A glass beaker shattered under him. He grunted then fell silent.

I could still hear the crackle of magic behind me but couldn't look. The fall had brought me to my knees and the pain was making me nauseous. I tried to ignore it, but I couldn't move my legs. I could barely breathe for the agony.

As the pain faded, I reached for the druid's head and tried to sense life. There was a faint pulse of magic, growing stronger as I held contact. These vampires had somehow made the bodies stronger than they should be. I struggled to turn the body and find a rope before he woke. As I tied his hands and feet, he gained consciousness. I had nothing to stuff in his mouth to silence him. I shucked my jacket and pulled my shirt off, creating a gag.

That one neutralized, I turned to help Trahaearn. He had a shield spell glowing in front of him and was defending against the fire balls that the final druid was hurling as fast as he could form them. The vampire druid was being drained by the use of magic, but not fast enough. Trahaearn seemed to be maintaining the shield well, but that wasn't going to get the job done. The sleep spell would be wearing off the other druids any minute. Trahaearn didn't seem able to attack, only defend.

I hoped he would be able to hold the vampire off long enough for me to tie all of the druids so they wouldn't be able to do any damage when they woke. But there was no handy roll of duct tape, or rope. I could gather the rest of the rosemary, pepper, and lavender, but before I could decide I heard a sour laugh from the vampire battling Trahaearn.

"You see, arch druid. You will be defeated by the hesitation of wizards."

I stopped dithering and looked around for another weapon. If I didn't have magic, I could still hit someone hard enough to knock them out.

"Do not worry about the wizard, vampire. You must deal with me," Trahaearn said. He cast a fireball of his own, but the vampire druid dodged. It wasn't trying to maintain a shield at the same time, which gave it the edge.

"He should have let the prophecy die," the vampire said. "We did all we could to stop it. Now here we all are. In battle, while the humans wait to kill us all."

If I engaged in the fight, I might end up damaging Trahaearn, or doing too much damage to the druid body. Even so, I could distract the vampire and give Trahaearn a better chance to finish the fight. "What do you mean, you did everything you could to stop it?"

"That child. We killed her parents to stop this travesty," he said, throwing his voice to ensure Dionne heard.

"It didn't work," I said. I looked over my shoulder and saw her standing in the archway. I held up my hand to stop her entering. This impostor was trying to bring her into the fight to cause a distraction. I waited until she nodded. Lionel stepped behind her and placed his hand on her shoulder. They both looked restored.

"You will not survive this," Trahaearn said.

"If you think you can stop us, druid, you are mistaken. You look at me and see a druid. You hold your hand because you do not want to damage this body. The only way you can win this battle is if Quinn Larson finds it in himself to stop us. He does not have what it takes. He was easy to manipulate. He returned the amulet to us. Do you think you will find it here?"

I almost told him that we didn't need the amulet to free the druid souls, but realized that he was trying to divert us. "Trahaearn, can you finish this? He's just hoping to delay us long enough for the others to wake."

"I am aware of that, Quinn," Trahaearn said as he lobbed another fireball.

I didn't understand how he planned to neutralize this vampire with a fireball. Surely if it made contact, he would burn.

"Okay," I said. "Get ready." I picked up a thick beaker from the floor. The glass was crusted with dust and slippery for it. I took a firm hold on the neck and hurled it toward the druid in the corner. He didn't see it coming as Trahaearn lobbed another fireball. I hadn't aimed to hit the druid, only to startle him, but he dodged Trahaearn's attack and moved into the trajectory of the beaker. It hit him squarely on the forehead, the force knocking him into the stone walls behind him.

Trahaearn dropped the defensive shield and stepped forward as the vampire druid slid unconscious to the floor.

25

"It would be easier to do this if we had the amulet in our hands," Trahaearn said as we pulled the false druids into a heap.

"Give me a minute," I said. All I could see was Dionne's face. She was staring at the druids. I could see power building within her, healing power that was twisted. Any healer could kill. I didn't want her to experience that so young. We would need all the druid bodies to house the spirits. I left Trahaearn to finish confining our prisoners. The first ones we'd overcome were starting to stir.

Walking to Dionne, I took her hands and spoke gently, "Where is Lionel?" I was hoping I could find some way to distract her from what she was planning to do.

"He's looking for the amulet," she said, not taking her eyes off Trahaearn's actions. "Do you think...? I mean, is it possible that they killed my parents? I know I guessed, but I didn't really believe it." She was trembling.

The power was still building, and I worried that she wasn't controlling it. That, instead, it was controlling her. I couldn't quite bring myself to lie to her outright. "Dionne, I don't know.

He was trying to make us fail, so he might have been lying. He was desperate."

Her hands were cold and getting colder. "He said they killed them to stop the prophecy. Someone protected me. Was it to avenge their death?"

We hadn't solved the mystery of Dionne's protector, but there had been someone looking after her safety. I wanted to focus on that. "We have a lot of unanswered questions. Promise me you won't do anything until we can ask. Dionne, please look at me."

She turned her gaze away from the activity in the lab. "Promise you'll find out. I know that the real druids didn't do it, but I can't stop thinking they should be punished."

The glow of power subsided, leaving her drawn, and me worried. If she was so quickly drained by drawing power, we would have to deal with it in her training. "I promise we'll find out."

She slumped, and I put my arms around her. "Come on. Rest here," I said as calmly as I could through my worries.

"Quinn, we need to get going," Trahaearn called.

I looked at what he'd done and saw the druid bodies lined up against the wall. He'd cleared an area around them and was walking toward Myrddin.

I coughed from the dust and the stress. "We need to discuss what exactly we are going to do." I was not going to just discard the vampires. As bad as their actions were, they were only trying to survive. "I don't know if any of us would have done something different in the same circumstance."

"Wizard, you are too soft." Trahaearn strode past me and started dragging Myrddin to the end of the row of bodies. "What they did isn't what any of us would do. They tried to survive at the expense of my druids. They killed Dionne's parents, and probably Inlackt's body. They did everything they could to misdirect you. And they allowed all of this sacred knowledge to crumble to ruin." It sounded like the last item on the list was the most important.

Looking around I couldn't argue with the mess. It wasn't just neglect; they were deliberate in the damage they'd done. "We need to talk to them." I nodded toward Myrddin. "He's probably the most knowledgeable. If he won't talk, we can try some others." I turned at the sound of footsteps. Lionel rushed along the hallway toward us.

"I couldn't find the amulet," he said. "If we don't have it, we'll take a lot of time to exchange the bodies. It will have to be one at a time."

"We need to be finished here fast," Trahaearn said. "The time we spend here is time we are not solving the results of the prophecy. We cannot hide forever."

"Stop." We were dithering. We were acting as though we were arguing, but there was no argument, just everyone stating what needed to be done. "It's not simple. So, here's how it is going to happen. Lionel, start making some confinement spells. I want those bodies held static without ropes. That way they can't do any damage, or be damaged." He nodded agreement and started digging through the debris for ingredients.

I continued giving orders before Trahaearn could step in. "Dionne, you're drained. I need you to rest. We will find your answers, but we need you ready to heal the druids as they return to their bodies. And right now, you couldn't heal a bruise on a mouse."

She looked ready to rebel but thought better of it. Instead of arguing, she said, "How am I going to restore my energy? You haven't taught me that."

I drew her away from the worst part of the debris. "Rest and I'll transfer some of mine."

Trahaearn pushed aside a pile of rubble. "Sit on this patch of earth. I thought Lionel said he would show you."

She obeyed him with no flash of rebellion. I was a bit jealous of that. "I told him we didn't have time for lessons, so he just fed me power."

"Then pay attention to what I do." Trahaearn placed his left hand on Dionne's forehead and his right on the earth. "They haven't tended the earth properly, there isn't much power here, but this is how you draw it."

Dionne frowned and then brightened. "I see it. Okay, I'll be fine."

"Okay, Quinn," the arch druid said. "What's next?"

There was no mockery in his voice, which made me feel confident. "We need some information. When Lionel has them confined, we need to get the truth. We need to get the amulet and transfer your druids. Do you know if we have enough bodies?"

He nodded. "They were very careful. When I was last in the amulet, I found twenty-one souls that needed to be returned."

"What happens when the druids are returned?" I hated the idea that the vampires would spend eternity in the amulet, but I couldn't think of a different home.

"I have enough confinement spells ready," Lionel said interrupting.

I looked at the handful of seeds he held out to me. "Okay, set them up." I left my question hanging.

We watched as he walked along the line of druids. At each one he cracked a seed between his fingernails and dropped it on some exposed skin of the target. When he reached the end, there were twenty-one rigid druid bodies. Each set of eyes blazed with the anger of the vampire soul inside.

I finally felt as though we had the advantage. "Can you give Myrddin the ability to answer questions?" I asked, as I walked toward the end of the line.

Trahaearn paced beside me. "I can ensure we get the truth," he said, darkness thickening the meaning of his words.

If anyone else had made that threat, I would have worried. I was confident that Trahaearn wouldn't risk the bodies. He cared too much about the real owners. The vampire spirits could be permanently damaged, but I vowed to keep him from doing anything that would harm them. "Let's see what we get without a spell." I was interested in what Myrddin would say to us on his own volition. Compelling the truth might lose us some valuable insights.

Lionel finished gathering a pile of dust. He sprinkled a few grains of salt into the mess and then blew it toward Myrddin's mouth.

"You will regret this, wizard," Myrddin sputtered. "Those druids are mad. You are better off with us in these bodies. We may be able to find a solution to this mess that the prophecy dumped us in. Something to save the Real Folk."

So much for valuable insights. "We are not negotiating with you, Myrddin. You are exchanging places with the real owners of these bodies. I promise that I will try to find a better solution, but you must leave the bodies."

"I will not help you to trap my brothers in that place."

I could feel Trahaearn's anger rising from his body. I glanced at him and shook my head. "Don't make this worse."

"Fine, I will wait until you are finished." He stepped away.

"Where is the amulet, Myrddin?"

"I will not help you."

"I can always send your spirits to the prison Fionuir has just vacated."

"You don't know how to separate our bodies and spirits."

"We did it with Lionel. It should be easy to modify the spell to send you to a different location." I was bluffing. Dionne had cast the spell, and I had not taken the time to study it.

"If you do such large magic, you will glow for days. Are you willing to stay in this place until it fades? To not do magic until the glow is gone?"

He was getting on my nerves. "I am willing to do whatever it takes to make this right."

"You think you are that smart? This druid will isolate the grove and let the rest of the Real Folk suffer rather than getting his precious coven involved."

I'd had enough. "The grove got involved before and look how you rewarded them. Myrddin, you are going to leave that body. You will either help, or you will be forced. I'm starting to think that we should treat you the way you treated the druids. Force you into the amulet. We are willing to do it one soul at a time."

"You don't have the guts," Myrddin spat at me. "Get it over with."

Trahaearn grabbed my arm. "He's up to something. We need to send him into the amulet."

I was afraid that Myrddin would do something once we placed him in it without someone to restrain him. I checked to see what the others were doing. Trahaearn was watching the druids carefully. Lionel was concocting some new charm. Dionne should have been sitting quietly on the earth, but she was coming into the room. She was angry, and by the pallor of her skin, she was still too weak to safely act on it.

"Dionne, stop." I stepped between her and Myrddin.

"No, he's doing something. I felt it through the earth. He's finding power somewhere." She raised her hand to cast something.

"Dionne, no," Trahaearn said.

I turned back to see what Myrddin was doing. He was mumbling and I saw power coalesce around him. Dionne came to a stop, struggling against an invisible barrier that Myrddin had cast. Her glow faded, and she started to collapse as the barrier began to suck power from her.

Myrddin was grinning and I knew it wasn't just spoken magic he'd accessed. He had somehow undone the binding spell. Lionel ran toward him, but Myrddin threw a fireball that caught Lionel on the shoulder and burned his clothing. He dropped to the ground stifling the flames.

"Come on, wizard. Show me that I'm wrong. Show me that you have what it takes." Myrddin was radiant with the power he was stealing from Dionne. Was he also trying to take her soul?

Trahaearn was reaching for the power around him, but Myrddin's spell was draining it as soon as he pulled it. Myrddin directed the excess power to the other bodies. "I'd like to see a spirit wizard break his vow. I want to see what price you pay for revenge."

I stepped forward into the path of Myrddin's spell. I needed to break the connection between Myrddin and the others. His spirit started to rise from his body. Now he was focused on Trahaearn.

He was going to steal the arch druid's body. No matter how powerful Trahaearn was, Myrddin had found a way to overwhelm him. My body became numb. I could feel myself mouthing an incantation that I had sworn never to use. One I'd learned an age ago from my master. One I had forgotten I knew.

I couldn't stop speaking the words. Dust rose from the floor and swirled in the air. I was marginally aware that Lionel was struggling to his feet. I heard him shouting at me, but I couldn't understand what he was trying to say. Trahaearn was reeling under the spell.

My arm came up without my conscious effort. The words flowed from me. Myrddin's eyes widened. His mouth stopped moving, and I saw his spirit start to retreat back into the body.

I heard a high-pitched scream as the spell left my hand to fly toward Myrddin. Then the scream multiplied and it was as if The Morrigan had join us. I fell to the ground, trying to block out the sound by covering my ears.

It didn't work. The noise was inside my head.

Then there was no sound. I could hear my heart beating, so I knew I wasn't deaf. Then I heard words. My name in different voices.

"Quinn," Dionne's voice cut through the confusion. "It's okay. You've ejected them, but the bodies are fine. You can look."

I could feel her healing power warm my spirit. I opened my eyes to see three faces staring back at me, worry creasing their brows. I pushed myself up and looked over at the bodies. They were lying limp and empty. There were no spirits in them. No glow. No power.

"Is it too late? Can we still save them?" If I'd killed his druids, I don't know that Trahaearn would be able to forgive me.

He knelt beside the body that Myrddin had stolen. He placed his fingers on the forehead and closed his eyes. "There is still time. We need the amulet. Dionne, can you do something to keep these bodies from dying?"

She left me and touched each of them. "I don't have the power to cast that spell over all of them. The bodies will die soon, but we have a few minutes. Maybe five. Probably not more."

26

Lionel was no longer standing beside me. He'd returned to the makings of the spell he'd been concocting before I'd done... well what I'd done. He returned with a handful of powdered herbs and minerals. I could smell the rosemary, pretty common to any spell. There was something bitter, like preserved lemons that had fermented. I saw the yellow of sulfur, and the deep red of rust.

He placed it on the closest table. "Give me a second," he said running to gather some twigs from the mess in the corner. "I know I should have waited until you gave me permission, but I made a spell."

"Don't worry. You are ready to do this." I watched him spit into the mess and then roll the twigs in the mixture. I didn't have enough power left to fuel a protection spell. "Trahaearn, can you contain it?" I didn't want to undermine Lionel's confidence, but we needed this to work. "I mean without blocking the amulet location if it isn't here?"

Lionel looked up without stopping his actions. "The spell will only have a range of a mile. I'm hoping the amulet is inside the museum."

Trahaearn took Dionne's hand. "Quinn, you need to help Lionel get it right. Dionne and I will link to power a dome of containment." He moved her to the archway. "Lionel, when you are done, what can we expect?"

He muttered a few words over the sticks and placed them in a line facing the hall. "The sticks will move and point in the direction of the souls in the amulet. It should lead us to them. You all need to follow me when I move."

"We don't have time to practice, Lionel, just start." I leaned in to hear the words of the spell, hoping I would notice if there was a fault in the casting.

As I watched, Lionel straightened, and then placed his hand, palm down, over the three twigs. He closed his eyes and then spoke what sounded like names. Three names, Gareth, Markel, and Berwyn.

The twigs spun in different directions. Was it something wrong with the spell? We thought of the amulet as one place, but when we were inside, I remember how vast it felt. By seeking the spirits, had Lionel given the spell too wide an area?

"This way," Lionel whispered.

While I'd been stewing over the possible faults in his spell, the twigs had aligned. Pointing toward the back wall, which was lined with bookshelves that butted up against each other. In the far corner where the fireballs had done damage to the books, there was one shelf unsinged. Trahaearn pulled Dionne with him and started to clear the shelf onto the floor, adding to the mess.

"There's no amulet here," he said turning back to Lionel.

The twigs were still pointing to the shelf. "Get closer. The spell is linked to you as a reference point," I said to Lionel.

He approached the bare shelf; the twigs didn't move. "It's here. I don't know how it's here, but it is definitely here."

He placed the twigs on the shelf and they swung to point to the far corner. I knew the amulet couldn't be there. It was about the size of my fist and would be obvious. "Lionel, what exactly did you set the spell to do?"

He slumped, losing his confidence. "I asked for the location of the three druid souls that I knew. Calling their names, should have sent us to the amulet."

Trahaearn stepped away from the shelf. "If the spirits are there, the amulet must be. If they left the amulet without entering the bodies, they would dissipate like the vampires just did."

"If there was a spell hiding the amulet, wouldn't it glow?" Lionel asked as he poked his finger into the corner of the shelf. He shook his head when there was nothing to be found.

"Maybe old spells don't count. Maybe it's only magic done since the prophecy that gives us away," Dionne said. She let go of Trahaearn and stood back. Hands on her hips, head cocked, she chewed her bottom lip in concentration. Suddenly pointing, she said, "Look, this unit is different from the others."

Trahaearn turned to look back at the druid bodies, seemed satisfied that they were still living, and turned his attention back to us. "I wouldn't expect they would match. We bring in new things as we need them." He pointed at the other furniture. "See, none of it is matching."

She ran her fingers down the edge of the bookshelf. "No, this is really different. Look, the sides are thick. Why would they need to make it with such heavy construction? Bookshelves aren't usually so bulky."

Lionel brought the twigs closer to the side of the bookshelf. They started to vibrate. "The souls are definitely here."

"Okay, get back," Dionne said. "Trahaearn come here."

She was poking and tapping the side of the unit. "Can we pull down the next unit? I think I need to get to the other side of this wood."

"Stand back," Trahaearn said before he yanked at the abutting bookshelves. The last few books fell from the shelves, bouncing off his head and shoulders. A cracking sound followed the books as the unit pulled away from the wall. Nails stuck out from the side. "It looks like they didn't want anyone getting at this," Trahaearn said as he reached into a gaping hole in the side of the shelf. Pulling his hand out, he showed us the amulet.

The twigs flew off the shelf and tried to impale themselves in the stone. "Thank you," Lionel shouted. The twigs dropped to join the debris on the floor.

Trahaearn ran to the bodies. "I need power," he yelled as he placed a hand on the first body. "Do not let me run out of power."

I held Trahaearn's wrist. Dionne and Lionel linked with me, and we poured power into the druid. If it drained us, we could replenish later.

This time we didn't join him in the amulet. I wasn't sure if Trahaearn even went inside. It seemed like he opened a portal and each soul found his own body. One by one the druids filled with something. Life replaced vacancy. They remained unconscious, but I felt less like I'd killed them.

As life poured into the last one, Trahaearn staggered. Dionne and Lionel dragged him to the uncovered patch of soil. I checked each of the druids and found strong pulses, and a flutter of consciousness. "Dionne, do you have any healing power left?"

She joined me. "They are going to need time more than anything. Remember Inlackt? I'll make sure the soul is settling in, and I think it best if I left them to sleep for a day. That way we can all replenish our strength and be ready to help."

I watched her gently touch each of the bodies. As she passed, they glowed briefly and seemed to settle into a deep sleep. "They are afraid and confused. I think, maybe some of them will need more than a little time to heal. Do Real Folk have psychiatrists?"

"No, but we have healers who can help." I saw the glow emanating from Dionne. "I don't know how we'll stop using magic long enough to be able to leave." I motioned for her to follow me as I returned to Lionel and Trahaearn.

"We'll help you clear this mess as much as we can. We have to do it without magic, or we won't be able to leave, ever."

Trahaearn looked around. "I wish I could offer you a better place to rest. But I can do magic because I will be staying."

"Can you find out what's happening outside?" Dionne rubbed her eyes. "And can you try to find out what's happening with Haruto, Herminia, Dai, and Tamrat?"

"I will find out what I can. Perhaps you and Lionel can search for some food, or a more comfortable place to rest." He waited until they were in another room before speaking. "I've checked already, Quinn."

"So, it's bad news?" My chest constricted with the thought that my friends were dead. "Tell me. If we know... I guess if we know the worst, we can find some way to live with it."

"Haruto and Herminia have gathered who they can, and found refuge in forested areas, much like we have here. Haruto says they will be fine because the humans in his area are closer to the old ways. The Real Folk don't exist in the cities, too many buildings, too little nature. Herminia, says that there have been some killings, but most of them are safe. She is hearing the same from her friends. Tamrat and those he knows are used to hiding and are simply retreating further. Dai isn't answering, but I sense strength in that part of the world."

"And your grove in California?" I asked, trying to delay the news about our friends.

"They report that the local folk are finding refuge in the grove or various communities in the hills. Also, that the humans are not clear what is different about us. It will not be long before they realize the truth, but they think it is a virus or some biological weapon."

"I guess no one has seen a troll or a kobold yet."

"There have been no killings locally," he said. "We were fast enough in our warning to protect everyone. Beacon has the fairies, imps, and sprites. The sidhe are all in the court. Mark is letting people into Banks', and a few are staying at home, not doing magic."

❧ 27 ❧

We stayed with Trahaearn until late afternoon, clearing the rubble from the rooms on the ground floor. We discovered that the living quarters downstairs were in better condition than the working areas. We carried the unconscious druids into the dormitory. As I touched each one, I wondered whether my act had really been against my oath, had I killed twenty-one beings, or saved them? I should have felt different, but perhaps the prophecy had changed the rules as well.

When we were alone, I asked Trahaearn if there was any information in the library that could prepare me for my punishment. He'd simply placed his hand on my forehead and closed his eyes. "You are still a spirit wizard, Quinn. The oath will take its price at some point, but I have no other knowledge for you."

Now we were at home, food in front of us, trying to figure out what we needed to do.

"You are a full wizard, Lionel," I said. "We should celebrate."

"No need. I want to stay here if I can," he said. "I'm not ready to set up on my own. And I'm not sure we are safe on our own any longer."

He was right. There were more problems to fix than just

finding a way to hide our magic. We were going to live very differ-ently in the future. "You are welcome as long as you want to be here."

"What about me?" Dionne asked. "I can't go back to the foster parents. I'll do magic by mistake and then... well whatever it won't be good."

"You can have the room upstairs," I said. "Between the desks and the couch downstairs, we can create a bed for you."

She grinned. It was good that someone was happy.

The front door opened. I pulled a defensive charm out. Had the humans found us? Were they coming down the hall to kill us? Panic overwhelmed my common sense. Magic still worked, no one who didn't have my permission, could enter my home.

"It's me, Quinn." Trahaearn joined us. "We need to talk to everyone."

As he strode into the kitchen I noticed two things. He was fully recovered from last night, and he wasn't glowing. When we'd left him two hours ago, he'd been shining like a lighthouse on a dark night because he'd done all the magic to allow us to fade. "How did you do that?"

He looked at me then at his hands. "It helps to be a druid. I dropped my energy into the soil outside the grove. It's doing some good, and I don't have the glow. It's not a permanent solution; the ground can only take so much power before it starts to glow."

"If only everyone could do that, we'd be over this danger," Dionne said.

"How are the druids?" Lionel asked. "Have you been able to rouse them?"

He shook his head. "I deepened your spell, Dionne. They are healing, but not as quickly as I had hoped. I will need your skills again."

"Whatever you need," she said.

"Dionne, you can't make promises without my permission. From now on, you need to stick to the oath."

"But, Quinn, he needs my help."

Trahaearn turned away, a grin growing on his face.

"Yes, and you will give that help. You need to stop going outside the restrictions of an apprentice. It's too dangerous now."

"Yes, Quinn." She filled a mug of tea for Trahaearn.

He sipped and made a face at the strength. "Speaking of apprentices, I want to offer Lionel the opportunity to work with me in rebuilding the grove. Now that he is a full wizard, he needs to find a specialty. No matter what has happened to the world, that hasn't changed."

Lionel looked at me, but I wasn't going to make his decisions now that he was no longer my apprentice. He needed to start acting on his own behalf.

"Trahaearn, I would be honored to join you. I won't hide away in the grove. We all have to work together now. We need to stop protecting our own and start protecting the whole world of Real Folk."

"I agree," Trahaearn said. "In fact, I think we need to extend it to the humans. Whatever we work out as a solution, we can no longer hold ourselves apart."

I retrieved an old bottle of whiskey from the cupboard. I brought four glasses to the counter. Pouring a much smaller portion for Dionne and adding enough water to ensure she wouldn't feel the effects, I raised my glass. "To a harmonious future."

"We can hope," Trahaearn said.

DIONNE HELPED LIONEL PACK WHAT HE NEEDED TO STAY AT the grove. "I should get my stuff too," she said. "If my things are gone from the foster parents, then everyone will really think I ran away."

Would I always be reigning her in? "No, you can't leave until we know it's safe."

She caught her sigh as it formed. "Quinn, the best way to make us safe is to have everyone think I ran away. I'll be careful. There will be no one there right now. I'll leave a note."

"But what if someone sees you? A friend?" I asked. "If you are seen around town, won't they start looking?"

She pulled her hair back into a ponytail. "So, I have to stay inside the house until I turn eighteen? Like I'm under house arrest?"

This was rapidly escalating into a fight I couldn't win. "Not house arrest, but you can't be seen, and we can't use a glamour."

She cocked her head and thought for a few seconds. "So, you are only objecting because I might get seen?"

"Yes," I said, thinking that was the end of it.

She went to the coats hanging in the hall. Taking one of Lionel's hooded jackets, she pulled it on, rolled the sleeves to cover her arms, and pulled up the hood. Shifting her stance slightly, she suddenly seemed menacing. "See, you don't need magic to change your appearance."

Defeated, I looked outside. The sun was bright and there were no clouds to cast a shadow and reveal any glow she got from inadvertent magic use. "Don't do magic, and don't get caught," I said. "How much stuff do you have?"

"I can pack everything I need in a couple of garbage bags," she said. "No need for anyone to come with me."

I opened the purse where I kept a supply of human money. "Take a cab there and back."

She took the cash and made the call for the taxi. "We should try to see what's happening in the human world," she said. "Go on the internet and see what people are saying."

Trahaearn shook his head. "No need. We know that everyone is as safe as possible. The humans have noticed something is different, but I think we have a few days at least, before they catch on that it's important."

A few minutes later, Dionne's taxi honked outside and she left.

I didn't think Ms. Metcalfe would be calling on us again, but if she did, Dionne would have to have a place in the house to hide until we convinced the woman that there was no trace of her. I added that to my list of things to worry about. At least that was only for a few months.

"What next?" Lionel asked. "I mean, we could go to Banks', or we could try to bring people together in a circle, or we could do both... I guess it feels like we need to fix this."

I wished we could just bunker down. I really wanted to wait out the inevitable carnage. This sort of thing had happened in small scale before. The vampires were destroyed — most of them — when the humans took notice. That time it was because the humans had become interested in mythology. Then some had become obsessed. Then the power of the obsession had revealed the vampires to be real.

Applying that to this situation was frightening. If the humans saw us in all our variety, they would not let it pass. There would be no way we could let this blow over. It just wouldn't blow over.

"It's probably too dangerous for us to go to Banks'. I don't want to get trapped there. So, anyone have an idea of what to do?"

Before anyone could answer a voice called from the backyard, "Quinn Larson, open the door."

I looked to the location of the sound and saw a raven-haired woman standing at my back door. It was The Morrigan. Or rather, it was someone who looked like The Morrigan, a pale example of the vitality she projected in her female form. I opened the door and she slipped in.

It was, in fact, The Morrigan, but now her hair showed glints of silver, and she wore a shapeless dress of rough gray linen. I didn't have to focus on externals in order to keep my senses. "What happened?"

She glanced at Lionel and Trahaearn. "I miss it, you know. It has only been a day, but men do not fear me, or lust for me. My power is gone."

"From the prophecy?" Lionel asked.

She ran a hand through her hair, a gesture of weariness that tore something inside me.

"The age has turned. I will be gone soon. You will have someone else to collect the souls of the dead," she said. "There are already so many dead, and so many more dying. I am almost happy that I don't have to keep taking them."

I offered her tea; she shook her head. "I am not staying. I come to deliver one final message before I am taken by my successor."

I would miss our encounters. Uncomfortable as they were, I always came away from them feeling more alive than when they started. If we were going to get a new elemental of the dead, I could only hope they were as interesting as The Morrigan had been.

Trahaearn stepped forward and took her hand. "Tell us your message."

"There will be a solution to this. There will be death and fear on both human and Real Folk sides, but you will both survive. Look for the benefits, druid. It is you who will save this world that we thought was reality."

Her giving Trahaearn that message lifted a weight from my shoulders. I felt slightly guilty for that, but she was right. I wasn't the kind of person to lead through this. We needed someone who could make decisions without considering everything that could go wrong. We needed someone whose oath didn't constrain them from any options. No matter what I'd done to the vampire souls, I was still a spirit wizard, so that wasn't me.

Trahaearn didn't fear the humans, like I did. He was arrogant, and that was probably the most useful attitude with humans.

"I am honored," Trahaearn said. "Is there anything we can do for you?"

She smiled and kissed him. "No, I am happy to be going. I find I am tired. That is something I have never felt before."

She moved toward me, placed a kiss on my cheek, and stepped back. As I watched, she faded, becoming translucent, and then invisible. A sudden lack of air in the room had me gasping and the sound of a woman laughing tore my being. The new elemental wasn't a nice person.

Trahaearn clapped me on my shoulder. "I'll need your help, Quinn. I think we're in for a long and dangerous time. I am happy that there is a future. I plan to make sure we all survive to experience it."

WANT MORE?

The world has changed and the magical folk are betrayed by their own power. Can Trahaearn find a way to peace? Use the QR code to grab your copy of DRUID today!

Sneak peek next.

If you enjoyed reading Imbalance, please consider helping other readers to find the story by leaving a review.

CHAPTER 1

The flap of sandals on the stone stairs caught Trahaearn's attention. He turned to see one of the few sane druids descend. Rising, he moved through the gap in the salt circle to speak to the man.

"Why have you come, Gareth?"

Gareth kept his eyes on the ground. Since his spirit and his body had been reunited, he'd acted ashamed. There was nothing he could have done to stop the vampires taking his body, but Gareth carried the blame nonetheless. Trahaearn knew he would be healing that wound for a long time.

"There is a human male at our front door. He keeps knocking, and I fear he will not be ignored," Gareth whispered.

In normal circumstances, Trahaearn would instruct Gareth, and let him deal with the human. These were not normal circumstances, and it would be a long time before any of the druids would be able to deal with anything, let alone a human.

"I'll be there in a few minutes. Do not answer the door. Perhaps he will give up. If not, I will speak with him."

Gareth nodded and turned to climb the stairs. Trahaearn turned to get Dionne's attention. She had completed the circle leaving a generous gate and was waiting for confirmation that she could close it. He walked to where she stood holding the last handful of salt needed to complete the spell. She was glowing a faint amber, not enough to be noticed in full daylight, but enough to show on a rainy day.

He told her about the intruder. "What can I say to him that will send him away without making him more suspicious?"

She thought for a moment and then smiled. "Tell him something that will seem boring. If you let him think there's something interesting inside, he'll keep coming back."

Boring would be easy, Trahaearn thought, I just have to lie.

In the few days he'd been in Vancouver, he'd found a druid grove held hostage by vampires, and an ages old prophecy that exposed the world of magic to humans. Ousting the vampires and freeing the spirits of his druids had been the first step in dealing with the damage from centuries of vampire control in this grove.

He strode up the stairs to confront this human who was interrupting his efforts to get the whole Real Folk world organized to survive the humans. He shoved aside the dread he felt at leaving two relative strangers in the most sacred place in the museum. He had a feeling that allowing others to do magic in his home was the least of the things he'd have to accept in the coming days.

As Trahaearn made his way down the corridor leading to the front door, he heard the thudding of a fist hitting wood. Whoever this human was, he was strong. The doors were solid and thick, having that much of an effect should have taken a hammer. But then, perhaps the vampires had weakened the doors somehow. Another thing he would have to investigate, and more than likely, repair when this crisis was over.

At the door, Trahaearn looked around to make sure none of the druids were wandering the main floor. Most of them simply slept, healing in the comfort of rest, but a few had been found walking in a daze. It would probably be better not to let the human inside anyway. The less he knew about the interior, the less work Trahaearn would need to do to make his lie believable.

He smoothed his robe and pulled the sleeves down to cover as much of his tattoos as possible. He hadn't done any magic, so there was no glow. Taking a deep breath, he arranged his features to an expression that displayed what he hoped would be seen as concern and puzzlement, an otherworldly attitude to match his story.

Before he could open the door, the banging started again. When it was over, he pulled the door open enough to let him walk through, and then closed it behind him. "Is there something I can do to help you?"

There were two men standing too close to him for courtesy. They stepped back and looked him over. Trahaearn watched as they made their minds up. One was a tall man, fat layered over his muscle, bald, and bearded. His companion was short, wiry, and nervous.

The tall one spoke. "We want to know what's going on inside."

"I am brother Trahaearn, and who are you?"

"It doesn't matter who we are. There are weird things going on, and we think you have something to do with it. Staying behind these doors. You're up to something."

So, it had started. The humans knew something was going on and they lashed out at the nearest mystery. "We are up to prayers and meditation. I apologize, but we do not open our doors to those who have not taken orders."

The bald man looked over Trahaearn's shoulder. "How come no one ever noticed you people before?"

Trahaearn looked at the ground, knowing that his meek demeanor would melt, and his arrogance would blaze through if he met the man's gaze. Arrogance was necessary in an arch druid, and came naturally to him. It was not believable in a monk. "I do not know what has changed. We have been here for more than a century." He looked up as he spoke, still avoiding eye contact.

The nervous guy was twitching with impatience. "Just show us inside and we'll go on our way." He stepped toward Trahaearn, but moved back when he realized that the monk was bigger and in better physical condition than he was.

"We are not open to visitors. I must ask that you leave." Trahaearn stood a little taller, keeping his eyes averted from theirs. He tried to convey that he was capable of enforcing the words without being openly aggressive. It was a fine line, and he counted on the robes to add a layer of piety to the act. With most of his druids still in comas from the trauma of their prison, he couldn't let anyone wander the museum.

The bald man grabbed his friend's arm. "Let me do the talking. So, what is the name of your group?"

This man was not as stupid as he first seemed.

"We are monks of the order of Saint David. Our lives are dedicated to prayer for all of the creatures of the earth, for peace, and prosperity. It is time for prayers now, and I must leave you." He turned to reach for the door.

"How many of you are there?" the bald man asked.

"There are twenty brothers here." Trahaearn didn't like the question. Was this man assessing the strength of the opposition if he broke in? It would do him no good. The doors were spelled and only someone who knew the phrases, and had power, would get them open. "We will not answer the door again."

He slipped through the gap and spent a moment inside placing a spell that would deaden the noise of knocking. Then he added a spell to allow him to hear what was going on outside. The voices of the two men became audible as soon as he finished speaking the last syllable. Trahaearn checked the glow on his skin as he listened — the shine was faint but growing.

"We should get a crowbar or something and open it up." That was the nervous man. "There's no way this has been here for a hundred years. I bet it has something to do with the weird glow-ing. Maybe aliens are in there."

The other man said, "You're crazy. There are no aliens. We need to figure out another way. I think I know someone we can get to help us."

The voices faded as the men left the grove. When he was sure that it was safe, Trahaearn would go and strengthen the protec-tion from the trees. It was not possible to keep people away, but it was possible to have their minds muddled and misdirected enough to make them turn elsewhere.

He looked at his skin again. The glow was not fading. If he did work with the trees, it could be hours before he could go outside again. In this situation, it was more dangerous to be kept in the museum than to be found by the occasional human. And the two men would find them again. Now that they had been in the grove, the misdirection spells would have no effect.

Trahaearn walked to the stairs preparing to join the others in the summoning circle. He knew that this would not be the last time he was left with no choices before the humans were prepared to accept the Real Folk into their world. To live along-side magical creatures, if not peacefully, at least without constant massacres.

CHAPTER 2

In the basement, Trahaearn told Dionne to get ready to close the circle, asked Lionel and Quinn to get in position, and hurried to arrange his thoughts. If they were going to spend time arguing with the other leaders, they might as well begin.

Dionne narrowed the gap and stood with the last of the salt in her hand waiting for the order to complete the spell. "Anyone need to go to the bathroom? Grab a snack? Take a Valium?"

Trahaearn couldn't help the smile that tugged at him with her words. It was too easy to get wrapped up in the dire consequences of the results of the prophecy. A little humor would go a long way to ease the tension. "I think we'll save the mood enhancers for after the conference. In fact, we can crack one of the bottles of wine I found in the cellar as a celebration."

Her face lit up at his suggestion that she was going share in the wine. The human habit of keeping young people from alcohol made it more interesting to them than it should be. He was about to tell her they would water down her glass when the room went icy. No wind. Nothing other than a drop in temperature. Then, the air seemed to blaze with heat.

Trahaearn motioned for Dionne to sit and the others to

remain where they were. Leaving the circle open was safer than trapping them here with something that could be fatal. Anything that could enter through the protections around the museum was powerful enough to do whatever it wanted.

"Who has violated my protections?" Powerful or not, he wasn't going to let it lie without challenge.

A hissing laugh filled the chamber. The heat lessened from a lung blistering level to simply uncomfortable, and the hissing was replaced with shrieks, then silence.

"I am Kali," a harsh voice declared. "I am the bringer of death."

Quinn reached for Trahaearn's hand and muttered, "Don't anger her. We don't know anything about this one. She doesn't sound like The Morrigan."

Trahaearn shook off Quinn's hand. "I am not in the habit of annoying goddesses." He didn't know much about the Kali legend, but he remembered it was violent and bloody. And that she was hard to stop.

"What is it that we can do for you, Kali?"

"Blood. Death." The voice was hollow.

Trahaearn hoped that Kali would be more lucid if he kept asking questions. "We do not conduct blood rites here. Is there something else we can do to please you?"

A glow rose at the opening to the circle. It came with the sound of wailing, and a scent of blood. The glow resolved into a face, strong featured, dark hair, the tongue oddly protruding. "Kill the humans. I want blood. I need the strength it will bring."

This was going to be complicated. Defying the goddess of death was dangerous. Even Quinn had trod carefully around the last one. The Morrigan had, at least, reveled in the two aspects, death and sexuality — or fertility to be precise. This one seemed only to be interested in death. "We have yet to understand the situation. The humans may want to make peace."

A shriek of laughter was the only response.

"Will you give us the time to find our way?" Trahaearn didn't want to promise or refuse anything. "It is too soon for the killing to begin."

A grinding hum replaced the shriek. Then, "I will have blood one way or another. Do not tarry long in your way finding."

Had he just promised to cause a genocide? Trahaearn realized it didn't matter what he'd promised, if Kali thought he was going to kill, she would hold him to it. Another problem he would have to deal with, but not right now. "I will endeavor to reach an understanding before you return."

The shrieking rose in volume until he feared his ears would burst. Then the heat rose until his skin felt like it was blistering, and then the air filled with ice, pulling his breath from his lungs. Just as he was about to collapse, everything returned to normal.

They were alone.

"What the hell was that?" Dionne asked.

"Dionne, stay out of it," Quinn said. "It's beyond your ability to deal with, no matter how many powers you have."

Lionel touched Dionne's arm. "Finish the circle. Even Kali cannot pass salt."

Trahaearn wasn't sure that Lionel was right, but regardless of what Kali could or couldn't do, they still had to try to make peace with the humans. At least there was only one human species. There were twenty types of Real Folk residing just in the Vancouver area.

TRAHAEARN SAT UP STRAIGHTER TO EASE THE STIFFNESS IN HIS back. The discussion was going about as well as he expected. No one agreed, but no one was willing to actually disagree. It was getting harder by the minute to keep the sarcastic comments under control. It felt like the humans would have time to slaughter everyone before any of these people came to a decision.

They knew that there had already been a few killings. Some fairies in Romania hadn't hidden quickly enough. The local humans had burned their gardens, and the fairies, in fear of the sudden glow that emanated from the flowers.

Beacon, the sprite who led the forest folk didn't think he had a problem. With all of the fairies, sprites and pixies hidden deep in Stanley Park, he thought no one would find them. Maeve, queen of the sidhe, was certain that they could keep the court invisible. Mark was worried but had admitted that he had no idea how to solve the problem. He had been nominated by the rest of the Real Folk, the ones who had found refuge in Banks', the local Real Folk pub. It made sense, a troll had no way of passing for human, in fact, most of the people trapped there were the same. Those who could pass, had taken the opportunity to find a way home as soon as they could travel.

Dionne was doing her best to explain what might happen, but the fact that she was a witch who could use all of the powers didn't make up for the fact that she was young, and she had been raised by humans. Discovering who she really was and what fate held for her hadn't been as much a shock as Trahaearn expected. Unfortunately, her history was likely to keep her from being an asset in this company. Perhaps it would help when they dealt with humans.

Quinn spent too much of his time defending Dionne, treating her like she was unable to make her own points. Lionel just seemed to be more interested in observing than moving things along. Trahaearn wondered if it was a result of his time in the amulet. Only a few days, but he'd been trapped in that world twice in an effort to serve a prophecy that had dumped the entire Real Folk community into a perilous situation. Why anyone had created that horror of a world inside the Gur amulet was beyond Trahaearn.

He knew that the best way forward was to create a small

council who could act for everyone. It was the druid way for good reason. It had worked for centuries. The Arch Druid had a veto, but it was rarely used.

Finally, tired of wasting time, he motioned for Dionne to end what she was saying and let him talk. The look of gratitude on her face gave him a twinge of guilt.

"If we don't form a plan and act, the humans will act first. If we allow that to happen, the best we can hope for is to be tolerated," he said to the images in the circle. "Is that your goal?"

Mark's image slowly shook his head. "I cannot imagine people like me being tolerated. We are not attractive like the sidhe, not useful like the forest folk, or the fairies. Some of us are downright scary."

Trahaearn waited. He needed everyone to state their position. No more waffling. He intended to get them on a path to agreement so he could move on from discussing what they would plan to the actual planning.

"I do not wish to see my people used for their power with plants," Beacon said. Then he glanced to Maeve. "I include the fairies, although I suppose they are your people."

Maeve laughed. "Please do not say that in front of their queens. They consider themselves a people of their own. I am surprised they have agreed to allow you to speak for them."

"Queen Bud is here with me to ensure I do the right thing." He cocked his head as though listening. "She agrees with me. That the humans would use us for their gardens and farms until we are worn to nothing."

All eyes, virtual or physical, turned to Maeve. She was the real challenge to a cohesive approach. The sidhe were beautiful in a way the humans would not be able to resist. They could simply fade into human society, changing location only as it became obvious they didn't age. Magic was a tool that they could put aside.

"I think it is in our interest to live alongside the humans.

There is more opportunity for power that way." She smiled. "And I see what you are thinking, power is what we crave."

That sounded like she would bide her time until the sidhe could control the humans. Trahaearn would let the humans deal with that. His goal was harmony.

"There is one more thing before we move on," Trahaearn said. "We have met our new death goddess." He'd kept the information about Kali out of the conversation until now, knowing that it would distract the participants. But he couldn't expect them to commit to any actions without knowing how different she was from The Morrigan.

Maeve's image moved closer. "Why should that interest us? The Morrigan rarely appeared to us. Well, most of us. She did seem to have an interesting relationship with Quinn."

Quinn blushed and looked down. "I always found it flattering and frightening at the same time. But this new being is not The Morrigan."

"Well, tell us, druid," Maeve commanded. "There is little time to waste on information that does not lead us to a working relationship with the humans."

Trahaearn knew that Maeve would always challenge the council they were creating. It was the nature of a sidhe to rule not cooperate. "This has a direct impact on our plans."

He explained as factually as possible the encounter with Kali. As he did, the echo of her madness seemed to fill the circle.

When he finished, Trahaearn asked Quinn to add anything he'd missed. A druid usually didn't miss details in such matters, but he couldn't take the chance that a nuance had slipped through, one that would make the difference.

"I noticed that the emotions didn't flood us," Quinn said. "When The Morrigan visited, even when I was blind, I felt the rawness of death and of sex. This Kali is a voice and madness, but it did not overwhelm my senses."

Trahaearn asked everyone in the circle, "Do any of you have

knowledge of this being? There must be a legend attached. There always is."

Maeve spoke for the others. "The Morrigan was ancient. I do not remember a time when she was not present. It would be a mistake to assume that all goddesses of death are also ones of fertility, or that each has a legend. The Morrigan was a legend from our homeland. That does not mean that all of these beings will be tied to a Real Folk history."

"I think there's something else, too," Dionne said. "Kali is new. She may be learning her powers like me. It wasn't that long ago that I had no idea there was this whole world, let alone that I was part of it."

It was possible that Kali would grow more powerful, Trahaearn thought. "Let us hope that Dionne is right, and Kali's madness diminishes as her power grows."

"Time is passing, druid," Maeve said. "What else do you wish to achieve?"

A good question. Trahaearn knew the long game he was playing was to get the Real Folk more than surviving this change, but what was he still missing from this gathering? Perhaps it was simply commitment. "If we are all agreed that the goal is to find a harmonious way to live among the humans, then I think we are done for the moment. Otherwise I fear we will inadvertently provide Kali with her wishes."

Each of the attendees agreed that they would work toward harmony. Maeve, as expected, did not just leave it there. "I think, druid, we need to agree on the authority we all have. I am not willing to cede anyone the authority to place a yoke on my court, but I do see that we need a leader. None of us wish a return of the witch trials when humans can't tell a witch from a sprite. Nor do we wish a second massacre like what happened to the vampires. If we are to speak for the entire world of Real Folk, we must not bicker amongst ourselves."

"Queen Maeve, please feel free to call me by my name. I'm sure you wouldn't want anyone to refer to you as sidhe." It was a risk to speak to her that way, but Trahaearn couldn't help hearing a level of distain when she called him druid. Knowing that it reflected the previous inhabitants of the druid bodies didn't help him accept it.

Maeve's image narrowed her eyes. Whether in seduction or warning, Trahaearn couldn't tell. Nor could he decide which to fear more. "Very well, Trahaearn. Now what authority will we hold in your new world?"

It didn't feel right to be answering that question. It wasn't so much that he couldn't take control, that's what his job was as arch druid. But he didn't think they would let him take it without assigning any blame. Even blame for problems that they caused. "Perhaps we should all say what authority would be acceptable?"

Beacon snorted. "I am prepared to hand over any authority. I only ask that no one sell my folk into slavery, but that does not need to be said."

"You can make deals for those who are at Banks', but we will want to vote on it." Mark's words came out in a grind of stone against stone.

Trahaearn waited for Maeve to speak, hoping she would be reasonable, but Dionne spoke first, "You can make decisions for me."

Lionel echoed her words.

Annoyed at everyone's willingness to be led, Trahaearn turned to Quinn. "Are you crazy enough to agree? Since you are the only wizard left in the area who hasn't handed me far too much power, will you draw the line this side of insanity?"

Quinn laughed. "I'm surprised that you are fighting this so hard. I will let you guide our decisions, but not make them."

A warm laugh filled the circle. Maeve was finally adding her opinion. "I think you need to take the lead, druid. It is only you or I who are capable, and no one will trust me. Now that you have our words, what do you propose?"

He wasn't going to buckle under. This was too important for egos and games. Only a true council would work. "I propose we work as a small group; we make plans, and we make decisions together. It works for the druids; it will work here."

"How many of us would be in the council?" Beacon asked. "Unless Quinn is joining, there are four of us, and that is not practical. We need a fifth, or any odd number to ensure we have a tie breaker."

Trahaearn was torn. He wanted to bang their heads together. If they couldn't agree quickly on the makeup of the council, how would they ever make a deal with the humans? It had been a little more than a day since the glow had happened and it was only a matter of time before they would lose the thin advantage they had. The Vancouver area was populated with more Real Folk than any other place in the world. It made sense that these people lead the effort to build an accord with the humans. He only hoped that the humans would be as willing to agree as a people as the Real Folk were.

An old lesson came to him as though his teacher were in the circle with them. *There is always time to slow down, but never time to repair haste.*

"We need to take a break. I will consider what you have said, and I will have an answer for you when we come back together. Shall we say a half hour?"

Maeve smirked, an odd expression for such a delicate and regal face. "We are yours to direct, Trahaearn." Her image flickered and then disappeared.

The other images simply disappeared with no comment.

Dionne stood and stretched. "Do you want me to break the circle?"

He nodded and she brushed the salt aside with the toe of her boot.

"I need to be alone to think. I will not be long. You may want to find food."

THE WORLD HAS CHANGED AND THE MAGICAL FOLK ARE betrayed by their own power. Can Trahaearn find a way to peace? Use the QR code to grab your copy of DRUID today!

FREE EBOOK

Claim your copy of Spells and Other Charms when you use the QR code to sign up for my newsletter and learn more about Quinn and Cate's past.

ALSO BY P A WILSON

For more books by P A Wilson

Use the QR code below or go to pawilson.ca

ABOUT THE AUTHOR

Perry Wilson is a Canadian author based in Vancouver, BC who has big ideas and an itch to tell stories. Having spent some time on university, a career, and life in general, she returned to writing in 2008 and hasn't looked back since (well, maybe a little, but only while parallel parking).

She is a member of the Vancouver Writers Social Group, The Royal City Literary Arts Society, and The Surrey Writing Workshop. Perry has self-published several novels. She writes the Madeline Journeys, a fantasy series about a high-powered lawyer who finds herself trapped in a magical world, the Quinn Larson Quests, which follows the adventures of a wizard named Quinn who must contend with volatile fae in the heart of Vancouver, and the Charity Deacon Investigations, a mystery thriller series about a private eye who tends to fall into serious trouble with her cases, and The Riverton Romances, a series based in a small town in Oregon, one of her favorite states. Her stand-alone novels are Breaking the Bonds, Closing the Circle, and The Dragon at The Edge of The Map.

For more information
www.pawilson.ca
pawilson@pawilson.ca

ACKNOWLEDGMENTS

People think that the process of writing is solitary. That's not the case for me. I have help from so many people it would be hard to acknowledge everyone, but I'll give it a try.

The support and inspiration I get from my writer's groups is incalculable. The Vancouver Writers Social Group opens my mind to other ways of telling a story. The Royal City Literary Arts Society gives me the opportunity to meet and share with other writers who have more knowledge than I do. The Other 11 Months group is where I learn about getting the words on the page. And my critique group who helps me find the best parts of the story I want to tell. Thanks to all of the members of these great groups.

Last of all, but definitely a huge part of the process, my beta readers. These are the people who love stories and are willing, and more than able, to tell me if my finished story is ready for you, my readers.